Children's Bedtime Treasury

Illustrated by
Jeremy Bays; Natalie Bould; Lynn Breeze; Anna Cattermole;
Maureen Galvani; Mary Hall; Virginia Margerison; Paula Martyr; Julia Oliver;
Martin Orme; Sara Silcock; Gillian Toft; Charlie Ann Turner;
Kerry Vaughan; Jenny Williams; Kirsty Wilson.

This edition published by Parragon Books Ltd in 2014

Parragon Books Ltd
Chartist House
15–17 Trim Street
Bath BA1 1HA, UK
www.parragon.com

ISBN 978-1-4723-7098-3

Printed in China

Children's Bedtime Treasury

Written by
Derek Hall, Alison Morris and Louisa Somerville

PaRragon

Bath • New York • Cologne • Melbourne • Delhi
Hong Kong • Shenzhen • Singapore • Amsterdam

Contents

Mrs Mouse's Holiday 6
Lucy and the Green Door 12
The Ugly Duckling 18
The Red Daffodil 26
Granny Casts a Spell 32
The Lonely Mermaid 38
Catswhiskers 44
Little Red Riding Hood 50
The King Who Ate Too Much 58
The Singing Bear 64
The Princess and the Snowman 70
The Frog Prince 76
The Greedy Hamster 84
The Very Big Parcel 90
The Enchanted Harp 96
Goldilocks and the Three Bears 102
The Chocolate Soldier 110
The Lost Lion 116
The Giant Who Shrank 122
The Naughty Broom 128
The Sad Clown 134
Snow White 140
The Magic Tree 148
The Bee Who Wanted More Stripes 154
The Invisible Imp 160
Ursula's Umbrella 166
Rapunzel 172
Buried Treasure 180

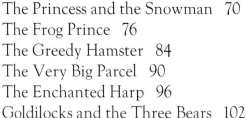
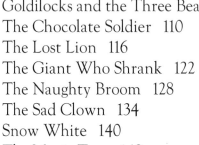

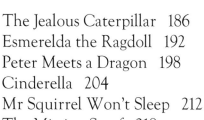

CONTENTS

The Jealous Caterpillar 186
Esmerelda the Ragdoll 192
Peter Meets a Dragon 198
Cinderella 204
Mr Squirrel Won't Sleep 212
The Missing Scarf 218
The Bear and the Ice Kingdom 224
The Toys That Ran Away 230
The Castle in the Clouds 236
Jack and the Beanstalk 242
Rusty's Big Day 250
The Wrong Kind of Puppy 256
Morag the Witch 262
The Dog With No Voice 268
The Three Little Pigs 274
Bobby's Best Birthday Present 282
Maurice the Minnow's Dangerous Journey 288
The Mirror of Dreams 294
Mr Mole Gets Lost 300
The Wolf and the Seven Goats 306
The Runaway Train 314
Little Tim and His Brother Sam 320
The Dragon Who Was Scared of Flying 326
The Mean King and the Crafty Lad 332
No Hunting! 338
Puss in Boots 344
The Golden Bird 352
The Boy Who Wished Too Much 358
Jimbo Comes Home 364
The Sleeping Beauty 370
You're Not My Best Friend 378

Mrs Mouse's Holiday

Mrs Mouse was very excited. All year she had been *so* busy. First, there had been nuts and berries to gather in readiness for winter. Then, she had needed to give her little house a big spring clean to make it nice and fresh. Now, as the warm sun shone down on the trees and flowers of her woodland home, she had promised herself a well-deserved holiday. But getting ready for holidays seemed to make one busier than ever! There was so much to do!

First, she took out her little case, opened it and placed it carefully on her neatly made bed. Then, she rushed to her cupboard and selected some fine holiday dresses. Back to her case she scuttled and placed them in. Now, she chose several pairs of shoes – a nice pair of sandals for walking along the front in,

a pair of smart shoes for shopping in, an even smarter pair for going to dinner in and another pair just in case!

"I'll need a couple of Sun hats," she thought to herself and so into the case they went as well. These were followed by a coat, some gloves and a scarf (just in case the breeze got up and it became cold). Then, in case it became very sunny, in went some sunglasses, some Sun cream and a sunshade. But, oh dear, there were so many things in the case that it refused to shut. She tried sitting on it and bouncing on it, but still it stubbornly would not close.

So, out from the case came all the things that she had just put in and Mrs Mouse scurried to the cupboard again and chose an even bigger case. This time they all fitted perfectly and she shut the case with a big sigh of relief.

Now, she was ready to go to the seaside for her holiday. She sat on the train, with her case on the rack above her head, munching her hazelnut sandwiches and looking eagerly out of the window hoping to see the sea. Finally, as the train chuffed around a bend, there it was! A great, deep blue sea shimmering in the Sun, with white gulls soaring over the cliffs and headlands.

"I'm really looking forward to a nice, quiet rest," she said to herself.

Her guest house was very comfortable and so close to the sea that she could smell the clean, salty air whenever she opened her window. "This is the life," she thought. "Nice and peaceful."

After she had put her clothes away, she put on her little swimming costume and her Sun hat and packed her beach bag. Now, she was ready for some peaceful sunbathing!

At the beach, she found herself a quiet spot, closed her eyes and was soon fast asleep. But not for long! A family of voles had arrived on the beach and they weren't trying to have a quiet time at all. The youngsters in the family yelled at the top of their voices, splashed water everywhere and sent their beach ball tumbling all over Mrs Mouse's neatly laid out beach towel.

Just as Mrs Mouse thought that it couldn't get any noisier, along came a crowd of ferrets. Now, if you've ever sat on a beach next to a crowd of ferrets, you'll know what it's like. Their noisy shouting and singing made Mrs Mouse's head buzz.

Mrs Mouse couldn't stand it a moment longer. She was just wondering where she might find some peace and quiet when she spotted a rock just a little way out to sea.

"If I swim out to that rock," she thought, "I will surely have some peace and quiet there." So she gathered up her belongings and swam over to the rock. It was a bit lumpy, but at least it was quiet. Soon, she was fast asleep again.

Just then, the rock started to move slowly out to sea! It wasn't really a rock at all, you see, but a turtle which had been dozing near the surface. Off into the sunset it went, with Mrs Mouse dozing on its back, quite unaware of what was happening.

9

Eventually, the turtle came to a deserted island. At that moment, Mrs Mouse woke up. She looked at the empty beach and without even knowing she had been sleeping on a turtle, she jumped off and swam to the shore, thinking it was the beach that she had just left.

Just then, the turtle swam off and Mrs Mouse suddenly realized what had happened. For a moment she was horrified. But then, she looked at the quiet, palm-fringed beach with no one about but herself and thought of the noisy beach she had just left.

"Well, perhaps this isn't such a bad place to spend a quiet holiday after all," she thought.

And that's just what she did. Day after day she lazed on her own private beach with no one to disturb her. There were plenty of coconuts and fruits to eat and she wanted for nothing. She even made herself a cosy bed from palm leaves.

Eventually, though, she started to miss her own little house in the woods and decided it was time to get back home. First, she took half a coconut and nibbled out the tasty inside. "That will make a fine boat to sit in," she said.

Next, she found a palm leaf and stuck it in the bottom of the shell. She took her little boat to the water's edge and, as the wind caught her palm leaf sail, off she floated back to the boarding house to get her belongings.

As she sailed back she thought, "This is the quietest holiday I've ever had. I may come back here next year!"

Lucy and the Green Door

Lucy Jenkins lived in an ordinary house, in an ordinary street, in an ordinary town. At the back of Lucy's house was an ordinary garden with ordinary flowers and an ordinary path. But down the path at the bottom of the garden was a tree that was not ordinary at all! It was a huge old oak tree and at the bottom of the tree was a very small green door, only just big enough for Lucy to squeeze through. This was Lucy's secret, because only she knew about the door. But what lay behind the door was Lucy's best secret of all!

Each afternoon Lucy would go down the garden path and knock lightly on the door. On the third knock the door would swing open wide and the chief elf would be there to welcome her inside.

"Come inside, little Lucy," the elf would always say, "and have some tea."

Inside, Lucy would meet some very special friends indeed! First, there were Penelope and Geraldine, two of the gentlest and sweetest fairies it was possible to imagine. Then, there were Basil and Granville, who were rather mischievous imps (but who made Lucy laugh with their tricks and jokes), and there were the storytellers, who would sit for hours with Lucy and tell her the greatest tales from all the corners of the world. And of course, there was the chief elf, who would make the most delicious milkshakes and scones with heaps of cream for Lucy to eat.

The world behind the green door was a wonderful place and Lucy would always go home afterwards feeling very cheerful and jolly. On one particular visit to the world behind the green door Lucy had just finished a scrumptious tea of cocoa and toasted marshmallows with the chief elf, when she went off to play games with Basil and Granville. They were playing blind man's buff and Lucy roared with laughter as Basil sneaked up on the blindfolded Granville and tickled him in the ribs, making him squeal and beg for the teasing to stop.

Now, just recently, Lucy had been feeling down in the dumps because very soon she would be going to school and would only be able to visit her friends at weekends. But they assured her that they would never forget her and that as long as she was always a true friend to them she could visit as often or as little as she liked. This cheered Lucy up considerably and then they took her to visit the storytellers so that her happiness was complete. Of all the delights behind the green door, the storytellers were Lucy's favourite. They told her stories of how the whales had learned to sing and of where the stars went when the Sun had risen in the sky and they had slipped from view.

Because of the assurances of the fairies, Lucy was not too worried when the day finally came for her to join all the other boys and girls of her age at school. Every day, Lucy would go to school and then afterwards would visit her friends behind the green door. As winter came round and the days grew dark she only visited at weekends and looked forward to the holidays when she could visit them every day once more.

Meanwhile, at school, Lucy had made friends with a girl called Jessica and although she told Jessica all about her family and her home, she didn't at first tell her about her extraordinary tree with the little green door and the magic world that lay beyond. Lucy did tell Jessica all the stories that she was told by the storytellers, however, and Jessica grew more and more curious about where she had heard all the wonderful tales. Every day, Jessica would ask more and more questions and Lucy found it more and more difficult to avoid telling her about her secret. Eventually, Lucy gave in and told Jessica all about her adventures behind the green door.

Jessica scoffed and laughed when Lucy told her about the chief elf and Basil, Granville, Penelope and Geraldine. She howled with laughter at the thought of the wonderful teas and the stories that followed. Jessica thought that Lucy was making the whole thing up! When Lucy protested and said it was true, Jessica told her that it simply wasn't possible – that there were no such things as elves and fairies and imps and strange and wonderful worlds behind doors in trees. Lucy was distraught and decided to take Jessica to the green door.

On the way home Lucy started to worry. What if she really had imagined it all? But if her wonderful friends didn't exist, how could she possibly know them? Jessica walked beside Lucy, still teasing her and laughing about Lucy's 'invisible' friends!

When Lucy and Jessica reached the bottom of the garden, Lucy was about to tap lightly on the green door at the bottom of the oak tree when she suddenly noticed the door had disappeared. She rubbed her eyes and looked again, but it simply wasn't there!

Jessica smirked and laughed at Lucy, calling her silly and babyish to believe in magic and fairy tales, and then ran off back down the road to school. Lucy could not face going back to school that afternoon and when her mother saw her enter the house she thought she must be ill – she looked so upset! Lucy went to bed early and cried herself to sleep.

And when Lucy slept she started to dream. The chief elf, Basil and Granville, Penelope and Geraldine and the storytellers were all there in the dream.

Then, Penelope and Geraldine stepped forward and hugged Lucy and the hug was so real that

Lucy began to hope it wasn't a dream! Then, they all hugged her and asked why she hadn't been to see them for so long and why they had not been able to reach out to her except now in the deepest of sleeps. Lucy explained what had happened on her last visit and told them all about Jessica and then Geraldine spoke. "Little Lucy," she said, "you are special. You believe in magic and you believe in the little people. And because you believe, you are able to see us and live among us. But those who don't believe will always be shut out from our world. You must keep your belief, little Lucy."

With a huge surge of happiness Lucy woke up, dressed quickly and ran out of her ordinary house, down the ordinary path in the ordinary garden up to the extraordinary tree, and was delighted to see the green door once more! She knocked very lightly and, after the third tap, the door swung open to reveal the chief elf. "Come inside, little Lucy," the elf said happily, "and have some tea."

The Ugly Duckling

Once upon a time, there was a mother duck who laid a clutch
of six beautiful little eggs. One day, she looked into her nest in
amazement. For there were her six small eggs but lying next
to them was another egg that was much, much bigger than the
others. "That's odd," she thought and went back to sitting on
the nest.

Soon, one by one, the smaller eggs hatched and out came six
pretty yellow ducklings. Yet the bigger egg still had not hatched.

The mother duck sat on the large egg for another day and
another night until eventually the egg cracked and out tumbled a
seventh duckling.

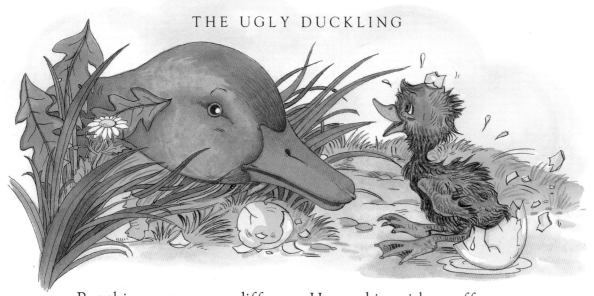

But this one was very different. He was big, with scruffy grey feathers and large brown feet.

"You do look different from my other chicks," exclaimed the mother duck, "but never mind, I'm sure you've got a heart of gold." And she cuddled him to her with all the other ducklings. Sure enough, he was very sweet-natured and happily played alongside the other ducklings.

One day, the mother duck led her ducklings down to the river to learn to swim. One by one they jumped into the water and splashed about. But when the big grey duckling leaped into the water he swam beautifully. He could swim faster and further than any of his brothers or sisters. The other ducklings were jealous and began to resent him.

"You're a big ugly duckling," they hissed at him. "You don't belong here." And when their mother wasn't looking they chased him right away.

The ugly duckling felt very sad as he waddled away across the fields. "I know I'm not fluffy and golden like my brothers and sisters," he said to himself. "I may have scruffy grey feathers and big brown feet, but I'm just as good as they are – and I'm better at swimming!" He sat down under a bush and started to cry. Just then, he heard a terrible sound – CRACK! CRACK! It was the sound of a gun. There were men out there shooting ducks. Then, only a short way from where he was hiding, a dog rushed past him, sniffing the ground. The ugly duckling did not dare to move. He stayed under the bush until it was dark and only then did he feel it was safe to come out.

He set off, not knowing which way he was going until eventually, through the darkness, he saw a light shining. The light came from a cosy-looking cottage. The ugly duckling looked inside cautiously. He could see a fire burning in the hearth and sitting by the fire was an old woman with a hen and a cat.

"Come in, little duckling," said the old woman. "You are welcome to stay here. For now, I can have duck's eggs each day as well as hen's eggs."

The ugly duckling was glad to warm himself by the fire. When the old lady had gone to bed, the hen and the cat cornered the duckling.

"Can you lay eggs?" enquired the hen.

"No," replied the duckling.

"Can you catch mice?" demanded the cat.

"No," replied the miserable duckling.

"Well, you're no use then, are you?" they sneered.

The next day, the old woman scolded the duckling: "You've been here a whole day and not one egg! You're no use, are you?"

So the ugly duckling waddled off out of the cottage. "I know when I'm not wanted," he said to himself mournfully.

He wandered along for a very long time until at last he reached a lake where he could live without anyone to bother him. He lived on the lake for many months. Gradually, the days got shorter and the nights longer. The wind blew the leaves off the trees. Winter came and the weather turned bitterly cold. The lake froze over and the ugly duckling shivered under the reeds at the lake's edge. He was desperately cold, hungry and lonely, but he had nowhere else to go.

At last, spring came, the weather got warmer and the ice on the lake melted. The ugly duckling felt the Sun on his feathers. "I think I'll go for a swim," he thought. He swam right out into the middle of the lake, where the water was as clear as a mirror. He looked down at his reflection in the water and stared and stared. Staring back at him was a beautiful white bird with a long, elegant neck. "I'm no longer an ugly duckling," he said to himself, "but what am I?"

At that moment, three big white birds just like himself flew towards him and landed on the lake. They swam right up to him and one of them said, "You are the most handsome swan that we have ever seen. Would you care to join us?"

"So *that's* what I am – I'm a swan," thought the bird that had been an ugly duckling. "I would love to join you," he said to the other swans. "Am I really a swan?" he asked, not quite believing it could be true.

"Of course you are!" replied the others. "Can't you see you're just like us?"

The three older swans became his best friends and the ugly duckling, that was now a beautiful swan, swam across the lake with them and there they lived together. He knew that he was one of them and that he would never be lonely again.

The Red Daffodil

It was spring time and all the daffodils were pushing their heads up towards the warmth of the Sun. Slowly, their golden petals unfolded to let their yellow trumpets dance in the breeze. One particular field of daffodils was a blaze of gold like all the others – but right in the middle was a single splash of red. For there in the middle was a red daffodil.

From the moment she opened her petals, the red daffodil knew she was different from the other flowers. They sneered at her and whispered to each other. "What a strange, poor creature!" said one.

"She must envy our beautiful golden colour," said another.

26

And indeed it was true. The red daffodil wished very much that she was like the others. Instead of being proud of her red petals, she was ashamed and hung her head low. "What's wrong with me?" she thought. "Why aren't there any other red daffodils in the field?"

Passers-by stopped to admire the field of beautiful daffodils. "What a wonderful sight!" they exclaimed. And the daffodils' heads swelled with pride and danced in the breeze all the more merrily.

Then, someone spotted the red daffodil right in the middle of the field. "Look at that extraordinary flower!" the man shouted. Everyone peered into the centre of the field.

"You're right," said someone else, "there's a red daffodil in the middle." Soon, a large crowd had gathered, all pointing and laughing at the red daffodil.

She could feel herself blushing even redder at the attention. "How I wish my petals would close up again," she said to herself in anguish. But try as she might, her fine red trumpet stood out for all to see.

Now, in the crowd of people gathered at the edge of the field was a little girl. People were pushing and shoving and she couldn't see anything at all. At last, her father lifted her high upon his shoulders so that she could see into the field. "Oh!" exclaimed the little girl in a very big voice. "So that's the red daffodil. I think it's really beautiful. What a lucky daffodil to be so different."

And do you know, other people heard what the little girl said and they began to whisper to each other, "Well, I must say, I actually thought myself it was rather pretty, you know." Before long, people were praising the daffodil's beauty and saying it must be a very special flower. The red daffodil heard what the crowd was saying. Now, she was blushing with pride and held her head as high as all the other daffodils in the field.

The other daffodils were furious. "What a foolish crowd," said one indignantly. "We are the beautiful ones!" They turned their heads away from the red daffodil and ignored her. She began to feel unhappy again.

By now, word had spread far and wide about the amazing red daffodil and people came from all over the land to see her. Soon, the King's daughter got to hear about the red daffodil. "I must see this for myself," said the Princess. She set off with her servant and eventually they came to the field where the red daffodil grew. When the Princess saw her, she clapped her hands with glee.

"The red daffodil is more beautiful than I ever imagined," she cried. Then, she had an idea. "Please bring my pet dove," she said to her servant. The man looked rather puzzled, but soon he returned with the bird. "As you know," said the Princess to the servant, "I am to be married tomorrow and I would dearly love to have that red daffodil in my wedding bouquet."

The Princess sent the dove into the middle of the field and it gently picked up the daffodil in its beak and brought her back to where the Princess stood. The Princess carried the daffodil back to the palace. She put the daffodil in a vase of water and there she stayed until the next day.

In the morning, the princess' servant took the red daffodil to the church. She could hear the bells and see all the guests assembling for the wedding ceremony. Then, she saw the Princess arrive in a coach driven by four white horses. How lovely the Princess looked in her white gown and her head crowned with deep red roses.

As the servant reached the church door, the princess' lady-in-waiting stepped forward holding a huge bouquet of flowers into which she placed the red daffodil just as the flowers were handed to the Princess. For a while, the red daffodil was overcome by the powerful scents of the other flowers in the bouquet, but when at last she looked around her she realized, with astonishment, that all of them were red. There were red daisies, red lilies, red carnations and red foxgloves. "Welcome," said one of the daisies, "you're one of us." And for the first time in her life, the red daffodil felt really at home.

After the wedding, the Princess scattered the flowers from her bouquet among the flowers in her garden. Every spring, when she opened her petals, the red daffodil found she was surrounded by lots of other red flowers and she lived happily in the garden for many, many years.

Granny Casts a Spell

Susie was very fond of her Granny. Each day, when Susie got home from school, Granny was always there sitting by the fire knitting. Granny knitted so fast that sometimes it seemed as though the knitting needles sparked in the firelight.

"Do you know," Granny would say, "that I'm really a witch?" Susie always laughed when Granny said that because she didn't look at all like a witch. She had a smiling face and kind eyes and she never wore black. Not ever. When Granny wasn't looking, Susie would take a peek inside her wardrobe just in case she might find a broomstick or a witch's hat. But she never found so much as a book of spells.

"I don't believe you're a witch," said Susie.

"I am," replied Granny, "and I'll cast a spell one day. You'll know when that day comes, for my needles will start to knit by themselves." After that, Susie kept a careful watch over Granny's needles, but they always lay quite still in the basket of knitting.

One day, Susie was playing in her garden when she heard the sound of crying. The sound seemed to be coming from under the old tree in the corner. She walked towards the tree and as she did so the crying noise got louder, but she could not see anyone there. Then, she looked down at her feet and there – sitting on a mossy stone – was a tiny little man. He was neatly dressed in a yellow velvet waistcoat and knickerbockers. On his feet were beautiful, shiny, buckled shoes and a three-cornered hat with a wren's feather in it trembled on his shaking head. When the little man saw Susie, he stopped crying and started to dab his eyes with a fine lace handkerchief.

"Whatever can the matter be?" asked Susie, crouching down.

"Oh dear, oh dear!" sobbed the little man, "I am the fairy princess' tailor and she has asked me to make her a lovely gown to wear to the May Ball tonight, but a wicked elf has played a trick on me and turned all my fine gossamer fabric into bats' wings. Now I shall never be able to make the Princess' gown and she will be very angry with me." He started to cry again.

"Don't cry!" said Susie. "I'm sure I can help. My Granny's got a sewing basket full of odds and ends. I'll see if she's got anything nice for a party dress. I'm sure she won't mind sparing some – after all, you won't need much," she said. At that, the little man looked a bit more cheerful.

"Wait here," said Susie, "while I run indoors and see." She ran up the garden path and in through the back door.

"Granny, Granny!" she called. She ran into the sitting room expecting to find Granny knitting by the fire. But Granny had her eyes closed and she was whispering to herself. On her lap was her knitting – and the needles were moving all by themselves, so that the yarn danced up and down on the old lady's knees.

34

For a moment, Susie was too astounded to move. Then, she thought, "I hope Granny's not casting a bad spell. I'd better make sure the little tailor is alright."

She ran back down the garden path and there under the tree sat the tailor, surrounded by a great pile of gorgeous gossamer, shining in the sunlight.

"I've never seen such fine material – ever!" he exclaimed. "But where did it come from? I just closed my eyes to dab them with my hanky and when I opened them again – there it was!"

"I don't know," said Susie, "but I think my Granny might have had something to do with it."

"Well, I'd never be able to thank her enough," said the tailor. "For now I shall be able to make the finest gown in the whole of fairyland. The Princess will dance the night away in the prettiest dress there ever was." He paused and then went on, "I'm also indebted to you, for it was you who helped me in the first place. I would like it very much if you came to the May Ball, too."

"Why, thank you so much," Susie replied, "I should like that very much." She didn't want to hurt the tailor's feelings but she knew she couldn't go – she was far too big to go to a fairy ball!

"Well I must get on with the dress now," said the little man, reaching for a pair of fairy scissors. "See you tonight!" And with that he vanished.

Susie went indoors again. Granny was knitting by the fire as usual. Susie wondered if she had dreamed the whole thing. Everything seemed so normal. Really, how could she have imagined she'd seen a fairy tailor in the garden! And as for Granny casting a spell!

That night, Susie lay in bed and wondered if the fairies really were having a ball. How she longed to be there! Once, she thought she heard a tapping at the window. Was that the fairy tailor she saw through the glass – or was she imagining it? In the middle of the night, she awoke with a start. There was a click, clicking noise at the end of her bed.

"Granny is that you?" called Susie.

"Yes, dear," replied Granny. "I couldn't sleep, so I decided to do some knitting. All at once the needles started twitching, so I knew it was time to cast a spell. What is your wish, Susie?"

"I ... I ...," stammered Susie, "I want to go to the May Ball," she blurted.

"Then you shall, my dear," said Granny.

In an instant, Susie felt herself shrinking and when she looked down she saw she was wearing a beautiful gown and tiny satin slippers. Then, she floated on gossamer wings out through the window and off to the Ball.

The next morning, Susie woke up in her bed. Had it all been a dream – the revelry, the fairy food, the frog band, the dance with the Fairy Prince? Then, she saw something peeping out from under her pillow. And what do you think it was? It was a tiny, tiny shred of the finest gossamer fabric.

The Lonely Mermaid

There once lived a mermaid named Miriam who was very lonely.
All day long she sat on a rock combing her long, yellow hair
and singing to herself. Sometimes, she would flick her beautiful
turquoise fish tail in the water and watch the ripples spreading
far out to sea. Miriam had not always been lonely. In fact, she
used to have a pair of playmates called Octopus and Dolphin.
Octopus had gone off to another part of the ocean to work for
the Sea King. He was always much in demand because he could do
eight jobs at once – one with each arm. Dolphin, meanwhile, had
gone away to teach singing in a school of dolphins. Miriam once
thought she heard his lovely song far away across the ocean and
she hoped in vain that he might come back and play.

One day, Miriam was sitting on her favourite rock as usual. "How lonely I am," she sighed to her reflection as she combed her hair and gazed at herself in the mirror.

To her astonishment, her reflection seemed to answer back. "Don't be lonely," said a voice. "Come and play with me."

Miriam couldn't understand it at all. She peered into the mirror and then she saw, beyond her own reflection, another mermaid! She was so startled that she dropped the mirror and her comb and spun around.

Miriam was puzzled by the sight in front of her. For there, sitting on the next rock was another mermaid – and yet she didn't look like a mermaid in many ways. She had short, dark, curly hair and wore a strange costume that definitely wasn't made of seaweed. When Miriam looked down to where the mermaid's fish tail should have been, she wanted to burst out laughing.

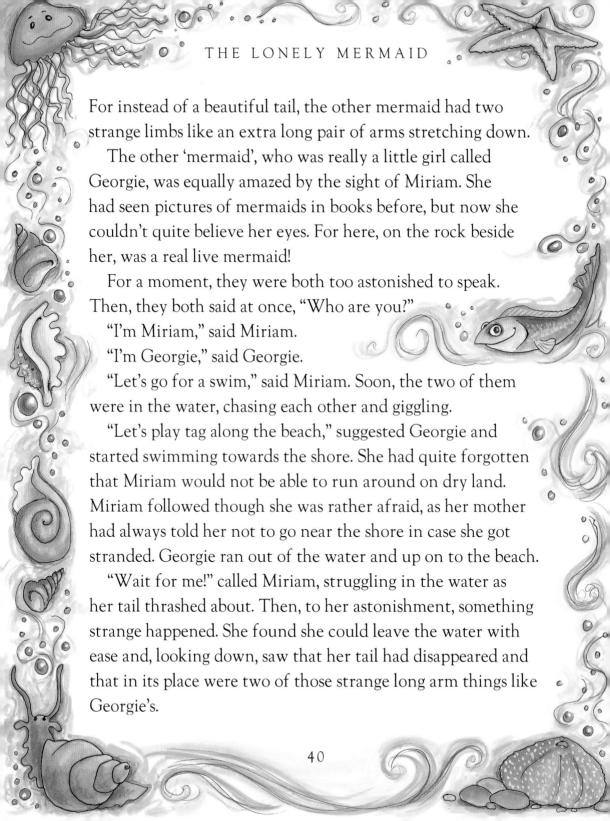

For instead of a beautiful tail, the other mermaid had two strange limbs like an extra long pair of arms stretching down.

The other 'mermaid', who was really a little girl called Georgie, was equally amazed by the sight of Miriam. She had seen pictures of mermaids in books before, but now she couldn't quite believe her eyes. For here, on the rock beside her, was a real live mermaid!

For a moment, they were both too astonished to speak. Then, they both said at once, "Who are you?"

"I'm Miriam," said Miriam.

"I'm Georgie," said Georgie.

"Let's go for a swim," said Miriam. Soon, the two of them were in the water, chasing each other and giggling.

"Let's play tag along the beach," suggested Georgie and started swimming towards the shore. She had quite forgotten that Miriam would not be able to run around on dry land. Miriam followed though she was rather afraid, as her mother had always told her not to go near the shore in case she got stranded. Georgie ran out of the water and up on to the beach.

"Wait for me!" called Miriam, struggling in the water as her tail thrashed about. Then, to her astonishment, something strange happened. She found she could leave the water with ease and, looking down, saw that her tail had disappeared and that in its place were two of those strange long arm things like Georgie's.

"What's happened?" she wailed.

Georgie looked round. "You've grown legs!" she shouted in amazement. "Now you can play tag!"

Miriam found that she rather liked having legs. She tried jumping in the air and Georgie taught her to hop and skip. "You can come and stay at my house, but first I must find you some clothes," said Georgie, looking at Miriam who was wearing nothing but her long, yellow hair. "Wait for me here!"

Georgie ran off and soon she was back with a T-shirt and shorts. Miriam put them on. They ran back to Georgie's house together. "This is my friend, Miriam," said Georgie to her mother. "Can she stay for tea?"

"Why, of course," said Georgie's mother.

"What's that strange thing?" whispered Miriam.

"It's a chair," said Georgie. She showed Miriam how to sit on the chair. All through teatime Miriam watched Georgie to see how she should eat from a plate and drink from a cup and saucer. She'd never tasted food like this before. How she wished she could have chocolate cake at home under the sea!

After tea Miriam said, "Now I'll show *you* how to do something." Taking Georgie by the hand she led her down to the beach again. There they picked up shells and then Miriam showed Georgie how to make a lovely necklace from shells threaded with seaweed. While they made their necklaces, Miriam taught Georgie how to sing songs of the sea.

Soon, it was bedtime. "You can sleep in the spare bed in my room," said Georgie. Miriam slipped in between the sheets. How strange it felt! She was used to feeling water all around her and here she was lying in a bed. She tossed and turned, feeling hotter and hotter, and couldn't sleep at all. In the middle of the night, she got up and threw open the window to get some fresh air.

She could smell the salty sea air and she began to feel rather homesick. Then, she heard a familiar sound from far away. It was Dolphin calling to her! The noise was getting closer and closer until at last Miriam knew what she must do. She slipped out of the house and ran down to the beach in the moonlight. As soon as her toes touched the water, her legs turned back into a fish tail and she swam out to sea to join Dolphin.

The next morning, when Georgie woke up, she was very upset to find that her friend had gone. When she told her mother who Miriam really was, her mother said, "The sea is a mermaid's true home and that's where she belongs. But I'm sure you two will always be friends."

And indeed, from time to time, Georgie was sure that she could see Miriam waving to her from the sea.

Catswhiskers

Catswhiskers was a pyjama case cat and a very fine-looking pyjama case cat at that. Susie's granny had sewn him together when Susie was only four years old. It had taken Susie's granny quite a long time to make Catswhiskers. Every night she had sat by the fire carefully cutting and sewing, until he was perfect. Catswhiskers' body was made from the finest black velvet. He had beautiful red glass eyes, a bushy tail and the longest whiskers you have ever seen. That is how he got the name Catswhiskers. Catswhiskers sat on the end of Susie's bed, looking at all the toys in the bedroom in that slightly snooty way that cats have of looking at things.

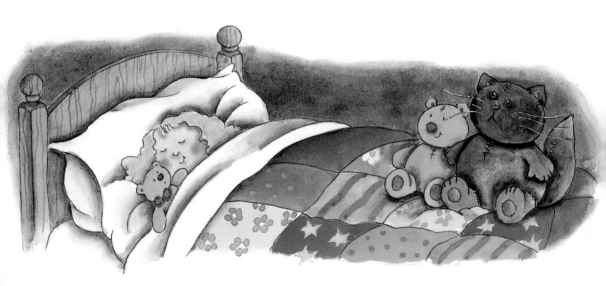

When Susie was asleep, or playing in another room, Catswhiskers and all the toys would talk to each other. But Catswhiskers was bored with talking to the toys. Jenny the ragdoll was – well – just a ragdoll. "What could a ragdoll possibly have to say that would be of interest to a velvet pyjama case cat?" thought Catswhiskers.

Then, there was Neddy the rocking horse. He was a perfectly pleasant rocking horse as far as rocking horses went, but he only ever seemed to want to talk about how nice and shiny he was and how he thought he was Susie's favourite toy. Even the alphabet bricks, the jack-in-the-box and the brightly coloured ball seemed to have nothing to say of interest to Catswhiskers. He sighed and looked at the window, wondering if life was more exciting outside.

45

One day, he decided he'd had enough of life in the bedroom with all the toys and that he would venture outside to see if he could meet someone more interesting to talk to. So that night, when it was dark and Susie was asleep, he crept carefully to the open bedroom window and jumped out. It was a clear, cold, moonlit night. Catswhiskers shivered a little to find it so cold outside and he maybe shivered a little more because he was also rather frightened. But he was very excited to be in the outside world, too, and he soon forgot about the cold and his fear.

He walked along the fence to the end of Susie's garden and jumped down into the garden next door. He had no sooner landed when he heard a fierce growl and saw two big, black eyes glinting in the moonlight.

It was Barker, next door's dog – and he didn't like cats at all. With a loud bark, Barker came rushing towards Catswhiskers. His mouth was open wide and Catswhiskers could see his big, sharp teeth. In fact, he thought that he could see all the way down into Barker's stomach! Catswhiskers only just had time to leap back on to the fence as Barker, jaws still snapping, gave chase.

"Phew, what a narrow escape," gasped Catswhiskers. "I didn't realize dogs were so unfriendly!"

He was wondering where it might be safe to go next when he heard a low, hissing voice behind him. "Hey, velvet cat," hissed the voice. "What do you think you are doing on *our* patch?"

Catswhiskers turned round to see the biggest, meanest-looking cat he had ever set eyes on. And behind *him* were several more mean-looking cats, all coming slowly towards Catswhiskers with their sharp claws at the ready. Catswhiskers didn't wait a second longer. He simply ran for his life.

Now, he was very frightened. He was also feeling cold and hungry. He wished that he was still in the warm safety of Susie's bedroom with the other toys. Just as he was thinking that the outside world was perhaps a bit *too* exciting, he heard the sound of a van approaching. It suddenly stopped, its glaring headlights shining straight at him. On the side of the van were the words STRAY CAT CATCHER.

Out of the van stepped a man carrying a big net. Catswhiskers thought he knew just who that net was for and decided that it was definitely time to go!

Without thinking about the dangers he might find himself in if he came face to face again with gangs of sharp-clawed cats or fierce, barking dogs, he ran back towards Susie's house as fast as his velvet legs could carry him. At last, he reached the window and jumped thankfully back inside.

Snuggled down again on the warm bed with all his familiar friends around him, Catswhiskers decided that perhaps this was the best life for a pyjama case cat after all.

Little Red Riding Hood

There was once a little girl who was given a lovely, bright red cloak by her grandmother. The little girl loved this cloak very much. She loved it so much in fact that she never wanted to take it off and was always wearing it. Because of this, she became known as Little Red Riding Hood.

One sunny morning, Little Red Riding Hood's mother asked her if she would take some cakes and apple juice to her grandmother, who was ill.

Little Red Riding Hood loved her grandmother very much and was pleased to be going to visit her.

"But don't delay," said Little Red Riding Hood's mother, "go straight to your grandmother's house and don't play in the forest on the way."

Little Red Riding Hood promised to do as she was told and said goodbye to her mother and set off.

On the way to her grandmother's house, Little Red Riding Hood met a wolf walking through the forest. Now, Little Red Riding Hood did not know that he was wicked and so she said, "Good morning, Mr Wolf."

"Well, good morning, Little Red Riding Hood," replied the wolf, "and where are you going?"

"I am going to visit my grandmother, who is ill in bed," said Little Red Riding Hood.

"What have you got in your basket, Little Red Riding Hood?" asked the wolf.

"I've got some cakes and a jug of apple juice," said Little Red Riding Hood.

"And where does your grandmother live?" asked the wolf.

"She lives in the forest, not far from here," said Little Red Riding Hood. "Her house is easy to find. It's right next to the lake."

Now, the reason that the wolf was asking all these questions was because he really wanted to gobble up Little Red Riding Hood and her grandmother. Suddenly, he thought of a cunning plan. "Little Red Riding Hood," he said, "I have an idea! Why don't you pick some of those beautiful flowers that are growing in the forest and give them to your sick grandmother?"

"What a good idea," said Little Red Riding Hood. "My grandmother would be so pleased to have some of these pretty flowers. I'm sure they would make her feel better."

And with that, she set about picking a big bunch of the prettiest flowers she could find. In fact, she was so busy looking for flowers that she didn't see the crafty wolf skip away and make off towards her grandmother's house. The wolf soon came to the house and knocked on the door.

"Who is it?" said Grandmother.

"It's me, Little Red Riding Hood," said the wolf. "I've brought you some cakes and a jug of apple juice."

"Come in, come in, my dear," said Grandmother, "the door isn't locked."

The wolf then went into the house and as soon as he saw the old lady lying in bed, he ran straight over to her and gobbled her up. Next, he put on her nightdress and her frilly night cap and jumped into her bed, pulling the bedclothes up to his chin.

In a little while, Little Red Riding Hood – who had by now picked a lovely bunch of flowers for her grandmother – came hurrying up the garden path. The door to her grandmother's house was still open and so she went inside and walked over to the bed. Little Red Riding Hood could only see a little bit of her face poking out from the bedclothes.

"My, Grandmother, what big ears you have," said Little Red Riding Hood.

54

"All the better to hear you with, my dear," said the wolf.

"My, Grandmother, what big eyes you have," said Little Red Riding Hood.

"All the better to see you with, my dear," said the wolf.

"My, Grandmother, what big hands you have," said Little Red Riding Hood.

"All the better to hold you tight with, my dear," said the wolf.

"My, Grandmother, what big teeth you have," said Little Red Riding Hood.

"All the better to eat you with, my dear," cried the wolf. And with that he jumped out of bed and gobbled her up.

The wolf felt very full and rather sleepy after he had eaten Little Red Riding Hood. After all, he'd already just eaten her grandmother, too. So he went back to bed and fell asleep, snoring loudly.

Just then, a hunter was passing the house and heard the snoring. He looked through the window and when he saw the wolf lying in bed, he realized that the wolf must have eaten the old lady. So, while the wolf was still sleeping, the hunter took his knife and cut open the wolf's stomach. To the hunter's great surprise, out popped Little Red Riding Hood and her grandmother. Luckily, the hunter had arrived just in time and both were still alive.

Little Red Riding Hood and her grandmother both thanked the hunter for saving them.

Little Red Riding Hood's grandmother ate the cakes and drank the apple juice and soon she was feeling much better. And Little Red Riding Hood? Well, she decided that she would never talk to a wolf again!

The King Who Ate Too Much

Long ago, in a kingdom far, far away, there lived a greedy king. Now, the thing that this King loved, more than anything else in the whole world, was food. He simply couldn't get enough of it. Ever since he was a little prince, he had been allowed to eat whatever he wanted, whenever he wanted it. And because he was always eating, he just got fatter and fatter and fatter with every day that passed.

When he became king, his appetite seemed to get even bigger! As soon as he woke in the morning, he would have his servants bring him an enormous breakfast. After eating several huge, steaming bowls of porridge, he would eat slice after slice of hot, buttered toast and jam, followed by all the boiled eggs that the royal chickens could lay.

In case he got a little hungry mid-morning, he would have a snack – usually ten or more chocolate cakes, washed down with as many cups of tea!

At lunchtime, the table would groan with the weight of all the pies, sandwiches, fruit and biscuits that the greedy King was about to gobble down.

For afternoon tea, it would be cakes, cakes and more cakes.

But the King's biggest meal was supper! The royal cooks toiled for most of the day to prepare this feast. When it was time for the King to eat, one servant after another would carry in great bowls of steaming soup, plates of fish of every kind, followed by huge roasts and dishes of vegetables. Down it all went, followed by fruit and jam. At last, the King would be full and he would retire to his bed for the night.

But the King's greedy eating habits also made him a very thoughtless king. No one dared tell him that much of the wealth of the kingdom had to be spent on his huge meals. In the meantime, his loyal subjects were going hungry and becoming poor and needy.

One day, just after the King had eaten his usual big lunch, he began to feel very strange. Not only did he feel even bigger than usual, he also began to feel very light. Suddenly, without any warning, he started floating up from the table and into the air like a big balloon.

"Help! Get me down!" he cried.

60

The royal courtiers and servants jumped up and down and tried in vain to grab the King as he floated upwards, but in no time at all he had floated out of reach. Before anyone knew it, he had floated out of the castle window. Out across the royal grounds he went, over the river and towards the woods and mountains of his kingdom.

"Wooaa-aaah!" cried the King, as he disappeared from view.

Soon, the King began to float over a small farm. He looked down and saw the farmer's children, dressed only in rags, searching for firewood. Some thin, hungry cows stood nearby chewing on a few meagre pieces of hay.

Over the next farm he floated and a similar sad scene met his gaze. Dressed in rags, a poor farmer and his family toiled their soil hoping to grow enough to eat.

Next, he floated over a small village. Everywhere he looked he saw shabby, run-down houses in need of repair and people in the streets begging for money.

Every farm and every village the King floated over told the same story of hunger and misery. The King suddenly felt very sad and very ashamed. He had been so busy enjoying himself eating that he hadn't given a thought to the plight of his subjects. While he was getting fatter and fatter, they were all getting thinner and poorer.

Now, a gust of wind was blowing the King back towards his castle. As he was passing over the castle, he suddenly felt himself falling. Down, down, he went until he landed back into the castle grounds with a great thud and a bounce.

That very day, the King sent out a royal proclamation. All his loyal subjects were to come to the castle for a huge feast, after which they would all be given a purse full of gold.

As for the King, he was never greedy again. Instead of spending all his money on food for himself, he gave enough to all the people in the land so that they would never be hungry or poor again.

63

The Singing Bear

Long ago, there lived a young boy named Peter. He was a gentle lad who loved all creatures, but most of all he loved the animals and birds of the forest. Many a time he had mended a jay's broken wing, or set a badger free from a cruel trap.

One day, the fair came to town and Peter was very excited. He could see brightly coloured tents being put up in the field and carts arriving with mysterious looking loads. As soon as the fair was open, Peter was off with his penny in his pocket to try his luck. First of all, he had a go at the coconut shy. Then, he tried to climb the greasy pole. Finally, he used his last farthing on the tombola stall. He was about to head for home when out of the corner of his eye he caught a glimpse of a dreadful sight. Lying in a cage, looking sad and forlorn, was a large brown bear. On a small plate at the front of the cage was the bear's name: Lombard. He looked so dejected that Peter immediately vowed to set him free. The cage was strongly padlocked and Peter knew not how he could break the lock. He turned to make his way home, with the bear gazing pitifully after him.

That night, Peter tossed and turned in his bed. What was he to do? He wasn't strong enough to break into the bear's cage and his keeper would surely not agree to set him free. In the middle of the night, he resolved to return to the fairground to comfort the bear.

He slipped out of bed and made his way by the light of the Moon back to the fairground. To his astonishment he found the bear singing a song to himself in a beautiful voice. For a while Peter listened to the lovely sound of the bear's singing. Then, he had an idea. He remembered a piece of paper he had seen pinned to the palace gate.

"Don't cry, Lombard," he said. "I think I know a way to get you out of here. But first you must teach me your song." The bear was happy to oblige and soon the two of them were singing the song together. Then, Peter said, "I must go, but I'll be back tomorrow. And remember, when you see me, be ready to sing your song."

The next day, Peter put on his very best clothes and set off for the palace. Pinned to the gate was the piece of paper, just as Peter had remembered. On the paper was written in a

handsome script: *The King Requires a Minstrel with a Fine Voice. Apply Within.*

Peter knocked at the gate. He was shown into a beautiful golden gallery where a row of minstrels were waiting to be auditioned. A courtier rang a little bell for silence and in came the King. He sat down at his great gold throne.

"Let the audition begin," cried the King. The first minstrel stepped forward. He sang a song in a sweet, high voice that tugged at the heart and reduced the court to tears. The next minstrel sang in a deep, rich voice that sent shivers down the spine, so that the birds in the trees stopped singing to listen. The next minstrel sang a song that was so witty and amusing that the entire court wept with laughter.

At last, it was Peter's turn. He stepped forward, gave a deep bow and said, "I beg Your Majesty's permission to perform my song out of doors, so that all the wild creatures of the forest might hear it, too."

"What a strange request!" said the King. However, if the truth be told, he had grown quite sleepy listening to so many beautiful songs and thought the fresh air might liven him up. "Very well, but it had better be worth it!" he said, giving Peter a fierce look.

The Princess and
the Snowman

One morning, Princess Bella looked out of her bedroom window
and saw that the palace was covered in a thick layer of snow.
Snow lay on the turrets and along the tops of the walls. There was
snow in the well and snow on the guards' hats. The palace garden
was so deep with snow it looked as though it was covered in
delicious icing. The snow looked fresh, inviting and untouched –
apart from a line of paw prints made by Bella's pet cat, Beau.

The Princess clapped her hands with glee. "I'm going to make
a snowman," she cried and rushed off to find her warmest coat
and gloves. Soon, she was busy in the garden rolling a great ball of
snow for the snowman's body and another one for his head.

At last, the snowman was finished and she put an old hat on his head and a scarf around his neck.

"Now," thought Princess Bella, "he needs a face." Turning to Beau she said, "Go and find the snowman a nose."

"Miaow!" said Beau and trotted off. Bella found three lumps of coal and stuck them in a row on the snowman's head to make a mouth. Then, she stuck a stone on each side of his head for ears. Beau came back with a piece of carrot in her mouth.

"Well done, Beau," said Bella. "That's perfect for a nose." And she stuck the carrot in place.

At that moment there was a call from a palace window. "Bella, Bella! Come inside at once. It's time for your lessons," called the Queen. Bella ran indoors and, do you know, she forgot all about giving the snowman a pair of eyes.

"I wonder when the Princess will come and give me my eyes," thought the snowman wistfully. "I'd better keep my wits about me." He listened hard with his stone ears and sniffed with his carrot nose, but there was no one there.

Night came and all the lights in the palace went out. In the middle of the night, a storm blew up. The windows of the palace rattled, the trees creaked and groaned and the wind moaned. The snowman strained his stone ears even harder and now he could hear a fearsome icy jangle and a piercing, shrieking laugh. It was the Ice Queen. As she blew past the snowman, he felt the Ice Queen's cold breath on his snowy cheek and the touch of her icicle fingers on his snowy brow. The snowman shivered with fear. Now, he heard the Ice Queen's icy tap, tap, tap on the palace door and her howl as she slipped through the keyhole. There was silence for a while, then suddenly the snowman heard a window being flung open and the Ice Queen's cruel laugh.

"She's leaving," thought the snowman with relief.

But what was this? Now he could hear the sound of a girl sobbing and as the Ice Queen passed he heard

Princess Bella's voice calling, "Help me!" Then, there was silence again, save for the sound of the wind in the trees.

"She's carried off the Princess," thought the snowman. "There's only one thing to do!" He drew his breath and with all his might he shouted through his coal lips, "Heeelp!" He thought to himself, "No one will hear my shouts above the noise of the wind."

But soon, he felt a warm glow on his cheek. "Can I help?" said a soft, kindly voice. "I am the South Wind and I can see you're in trouble."

The snowman could hardly believe his stone ears. "Oh, yes, please help," he cried. "The Ice Queen has carried off Princess Bella and I'm afraid she may die of cold."

"I'll see what I can do," said the South Wind gently and she started to blow a warm wind. She blew and she blew and soon the Ice Queen's icy arms began to melt. Then, Bella was able to slip from her cold grasp.

"It was the snowman who saved you," whispered the South Wind in Bella's ear as she carried her back to the palace.

Bella could hear the drip, drip, sound of snow being melted by the South Wind's warm breath. As she reached the palace gate, the Sun was rising and the snow in the garden was turning to slush. "I must see my snowman before he is gone," she thought.

There he was on the lawn. His hat was starting to slide off his head and his mouth was all crooked. She rushed over to him and to her astonishment he spoke.

"Please give me my eyes before I melt completely," he begged.

"Yes, of course I will," Bella replied. Quickly she fixed two pieces of coal in place on his melting face.

"You are so lovely," said the snowman, looking at her with his coal eyes. "I have one last request before I'm gone. Will you marry me?"

"Why, I will!" said Bella without thinking twice – for how could she refuse the request of the one who had saved her from the Ice Queen?

Bella could not bear to think that the snowman was melting away. She glanced down so that he would not see that she was crying.

"Bella," he said. She looked up and there standing before her was a prince. For once in her life she was speechless.

"Long ago, the Ice Queen carried me away – just like she did to you. She cast a spell on me that meant I could only return to Earth as falling snow. But by agreeing to marry me you have broken the spell," said the Prince.

And so Bella and the Prince were married and lived happily ever after.

The Frog Prince

There was once a king who had but one daughter. Being his only child, she wanted for nothing. She had a nursery full of toys, a pony to ride and a wardrobe bursting with pretty dresses. But, for all this, the Princess was lonely. "How I wish I had someone to play with," she sighed.

The Princess' favourite toy was a beautiful golden ball. Every day she would play with her ball in the palace garden. When she threw the ball up in the air, it seemed to take off of its own accord and touch the clouds before landing in the Princess' hands again.

One windy day, the Princess was playing in the garden as usual. She threw her golden ball high into the air, but instead of returning to her hands, the wind blew the ball into the fishpond. The Princess ran to the pond, but to her dismay the ball had sunk right to the bottom. "Whatever shall I do?" wailed the girl. "Now I have lost my favourite toy." And she sat down beside the pond and cried.

All at once she heard a loud PLOP! and a large green frog landed on the grass beside her. "Eeeuugh! Go away you nasty thing!" screamed the Princess.

To her astonishment, the frog spoke to her. "I heard you crying," he said in a gentle voice, "and I wondered what the matter was. Can I help you in any way?"

"Why, yes!" exclaimed the Princess, once she had got over the shock of being addressed by a frog. "My ball has sunk to the bottom of the pond. Would you fish it out for me?"

"Of course I will," replied the frog. "But in return, what will you give me if I do?"

"You can have my jewels, my finest clothes and even my crown if you will find my ball," said the Princess hastily, for she was truly eager to get her favourite toy back.

"I do not want your jewels, your clothes or your crown," replied the frog. "I would like to be your friend. I want to return with you to the palace and eat from your golden plate and sip from your golden cup. At night I want to sleep on a cushion made of silk next to your bed and I want you to kiss me good night before I go to sleep, too."

"I promise all you ask," said the girl, "if only you will find my golden ball."

"Remember what you have promised," said the frog, as he dived deep into the pond. At last, he surfaced again with the ball and threw it on to the grass beside the Princess. She was so overjoyed she forgot all about thanking the frog – let alone her promise – and ran all the way back to the palace.

That evening, the King, the Queen and the Princess were having dinner in the great hall of the palace, when a courtier approached the King and said, "Your Majesty, there is a frog at the door who says the Princess has promised to share her dinner with him."

"Is this true?" demanded the King, turning to the Princess and looking rather angry.

"Yes, it is," said the Princess in a small voice. And she told her father the whole story.

"When a promise is made it must be kept, my girl," said the King. "You must ask the frog to dine with you."

Just then, the frog hopped into the great hall and round to where the Princess was sitting. With a great leap he was up on the table beside her. She stifled a scream.

"You promised to let me eat from your golden plate," said the frog, tucking into the Princess' food. The Princess felt quite sick and pushed the plate away from her. Then, to her horror, the frog dipped his long tongue into her golden cup and drank every drop. "It's what you promised," he reminded her.

When he had finished, the frog stretched his long, green limbs, yawned and said, "Now I feel quite sleepy. Please take me to your room."

"Do I have to?" the Princess pleaded with her father.

"Yes, you do," said the King sternly. "The frog helped you when you were in need and you made him a promise."

So the Princess carried the frog to her bedroom but as they reached the door she said, "My bedroom's very warm. I'm sure you'd be more comfortable out here where it's cool."

But as she opened the bedroom door, the frog leaped from her hand and landed on her bed.

"You promised that I could sleep on a silk cushion next to your bed," said the frog.

"Yes, yes, of course," said the Princess looking with horror at the froggy footprints on her clean, white sheets. She called to her maid to bring a cushion.

The frog jumped on to the cushion and looked as though he was going to sleep.

"Good," thought the Princess, "he's forgotten about my final promise."

But just as she was about to get into bed, he opened his eyes and said, "What about my goodnight kiss?"

"Oh, woe is me," thought the Princess as she closed her eyes and pursed her lips towards the frog's cold and clammy face and kissed him.

"Open your eyes," said a voice that didn't sound a bit like the frog's. She opened her eyes and there, standing before her, was a Prince. The Princess stood there in dumbstruck amazement.

"Thank you," said the Prince.
"You have broken a spell cast upon
me by a wicked witch. She turned
me into a frog and said the spell
would only be broken if a Princess
would eat with me, sleep beside me
and kiss me."

They ran to tell the King what had happened.
He was delighted and said, "You may live in the palace from now
on, for my daughter needs a friend." And indeed, the Prince and
Princess became the best of friends and she was never lonely
again. He taught her to play football with the golden ball and
she taught him to ride her pony. One day, many years later, they
were married and had lots of children. And, do you know, their
children were particularly good at leapfrog.

The Greedy Hamster

There was once a hamster named Harry. He was a very greedy hamster. As soon as his food was put in his cage he gobbled it all up and then he would push his little nose through the bars in the hope that something else to eat might come within reach. From his cage he could see all manner of delicious food on the kitchen table – and the smells! The scent of freshly baked bread was enough to send him spinning round in his exercise wheel with frustration.

"It's not fair!" he grumbled to himself. "They're all eating themselves silly out there and here am I simply starving to death!" (At this point he would usually remember the large meal he had just eaten and that his tummy was indeed still rather full.)

"If only I could get out of this beastly cage, I could feast on all the food I deserve," he announced to himself and the thought of all those tasty morsels made his mouth water.

One night, after the family had gone to bed, Harry was having one last spin in his wheel before retiring to his sawdust mattress. As he spun around, he heard an unfamiliar squeaky noise.

"That's funny," thought Harry. "The little girl oiled my wheel only today. It surely can't need oiling again." He stopped running and got off the wheel, but the squeak continued. Harry sat quite still on his haunches and listened intently. Then, he realized it was the door to his cage squeaking. The door! The door was flapping open. The little girl had not closed it properly before she went to bed. Harry did a little dance of glee. Then, he went to the door and looked cautiously out in case there was any danger. But all seemed to be well. The cat was asleep on a chair. The dog was sleeping soundly on the floor.

Now, as well as being a greedy hamster, Harry was also clever. Once outside the cage, the first thing he did was look at the catch to see how it worked. Yes! He was pretty sure he could work out how to open it from the inside now. Harry sniffed the air. There were some tasty titbits left over from a birthday party on the table. He could smell the sugar icing and soon he was on the table, cramming his mouth with odds and ends of cheese sandwiches and pieces of chocolate cake. When he had eaten his fill, he stuffed his cheek pouches with ginger biscuits and ran back into his cage, closing the door behind him.

"Good!" thought Harry. "Now I will never be hungry again."

The next night, Harry let himself out of his cage and helped himself to food and again the next night and the night after that. He feasted on everything and anything – nuts, bananas, pieces of bread, left-over jam and slices of pizza were all pushed into his greedy mouth. Each time he returned to his cage he filled his cheeks with more and more food. He did not notice that he was getting fatter and fatter, although he was aware that he could no longer run round in his wheel without falling off! Then, one night, he undid the door catch but found he was simply too wide to get through the door!

For a while Harry sat in a very bad temper in the corner of the cage. His cheeks were still bulging with food from his last midnight feast, but the greedy hamster wanted more. Then, he had an idea. "I'll get that lazy cat to help," he thought. He squealed at the top of his voice until the cat, who had been dreaming of rats, woke up with a start.

"What do you want?" she hissed at Harry. Harry explained his problem.

"Of course, I'd be only too pleased to help," said the crafty cat, thinking to herself here was an extra dinner! With her strong claws she bent back the door frame of the cage, until there was just enough room for Harry to squeeze through. Then, with a mighty swipe of her paw, she caught him and gobbled him whole. She felt extremely full, what with Harry and all his food inside her. She could barely crawl back to her chair and soon she was fast asleep again and snoring loudly with her mouth open. Inside her tummy Harry, too, felt very uncomfortable. Every time the cat snored, it sounded like a thunderstorm raging around his head.

"I must get out of here," he thought and headed for the cat's open jaws. But he was far too fat to get out again. Then, he had another idea. Through the cat's jaws he could see the dog lying on the floor.

"Help! Help!" he squeaked. The dog woke up to a very strange sight. There was the cat lying on the chair snoring, but she also seemed to be squeaking, "Help!" The dog put his head on one side. He was very perplexed. Then, he saw a pair of beady eyes and some fine whiskers inside the cat's mouth. It was Harry!

"Get me out of here, please," pleaded Harry.

Now, the dog did not very much like the cat, so he was quite willing to help the hamster.

"I'll stick my tail in the cat's mouth. Then you hang on while I pull you out," said the dog. "But mind you don't make a sound and wake the cat, or she'll surely bite my tail!" The dog gingerly put the tip of his tail inside the cat's open jaws, just far enough for Harry's little paws to grab hold. Then, he pulled with all his might. Out popped Harry and out of Harry popped all the food he'd stored in his cheeks – peanuts, an apple core and a slice of jam tart!

"Thank you, thank you," gasped Harry, as he made a dash for his cage and slammed the door shut. "I think I'll stay in my cage from now on and just stick to the food I'm given!"

He carried it into the kitchen and put it on the table. Then, he took a knife and cut the fruit in half. To his astonishment out poured a pile of gold coins. "Come quickly!" he called to his wife. Well, the pair of them danced round the kitchen for joy.

The old couple decided to spend just one gold coin and keep the rest. "After all," said the woman wisely, "we don't know what's in the other fruits. They may be full of worms." So they spent one golden penny in the town and put the rest aside.

The next day, the old man picked another big red fruit and this, too, was full of gold. After that the old couple were less careful with their money, thinking all the fruits must be full of gold. They had a wonderful time buying fine clothes and things for the house and garden. Each day, the man picked another fruit. Each day it was full of gold and each day they went into town and had a grand time spending the money. But all the while the man forgot entirely to water the tree.

Meanwhile, the old couple's friends and neighbours started to gossip among themselves. They wondered where all the money was coming from and they began to resent the old couple. They noticed that the old couple didn't buy anything for their friends, or even throw a party. Gradually, their friends ignored them until the old couple were left with no friends at all. But they didn't even notice because they were so busy spending the gold coins.

Then one day, the old man looked out into the garden and saw that the tree was all withered. He rushed outside and threw bucket after bucket of water over the tree, but all to no avail.

He and his wife frantically picked the fruits left on the tree, but when they took them indoors they found to their dismay that they were cracked and gnarled. When they broke open the fruits they were full of dust. "If only I had not been so thoughtless and remembered to water the tree!" cried the old man in anguish.

The next day, the old couple looked out of the window to find that the tree had vanished. Now what were they to do? They had completely neglected to take care of their garden and now they had nothing to eat. They realized that they would have to sell their riches to buy food. Then, they also needed new gardening tools, for theirs had grown rusty with neglect.

As the weeks passed, the old man and his wife gradually sold all the fine things they had bought, just to keep body and soul together. They felt truly miserable and sorry for the way they had treated their neighbours. For now they realized just how lonely they were without their friends. "We have no money now," said the wife one day, "but let's have a party anyway. For friendship is more valuable than any amount of gold coins."

So the old couple invited all their friends and neighbours round and they had a grand party. The friends wondered what had happened to all the old couple's riches and what had happened to make the old couple so friendly once more, but I don't think they ever found out, do you?

The Enchanted Harp

Long ago, there lived a pedlar. Every day he took up the same place in the market square with his harp. Now, this was no ordinary harp. It was an enchanted harp. The pedlar would call out to passers-by and, for a penny, the harp would play all on its own any tune they wished. It could play any sort of tune from the slowest, most tearful ballad to the liveliest, happiest jig. It could play music for any occasion. Sometimes, a wedding party would come by just to have the harp play a tune for the bride and groom.

Now one day, a young man passed through the town. He heard the sound of the harp's sweet music coming from the market square and made his way over to where the pedlar stood. He couldn't believe his eyes or his ears! The harp was playing a lullaby for a lady with a baby that was crying. The music was so enchanting that the baby soon stopped wailing and was fast asleep. Then, he saw an old man give the pedlar a penny and whisper in his ear. The harp changed its tune and now it played an ancient melody that the old man had not heard for many a year and his eyes filled with tears of gratitude.

The young man watched all this and thought to himself, "If only that harp were mine. I could make a lot more money with it than that silly old pedlar!" He waited a while for the crowd to disperse and then when he thought no one was looking he went up to the pedlar and said, "People say that on this day a great spotted pig will fall out of the sky and land on the market square.

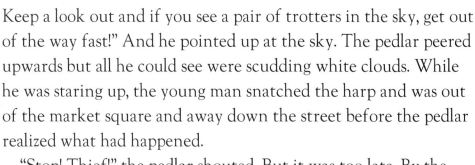

Keep a look out and if you see a pair of trotters in the sky, get out of the way fast!" And he pointed up at the sky. The pedlar peered upwards but all he could see were scudding white clouds. While he was staring up, the young man snatched the harp and was out of the market square and away down the street before the pedlar realized what had happened.

"Stop! Thief!" the pedlar shouted. But it was too late. By the time people gave chase the young man had gone. He didn't stop running until he reached a town many miles away, where no one had seen the enchanted harp before.

The young man set up the harp and called out to passers-by, "Two pennies and my harp will play any tune you wish!" A man and woman came up and asked for a waltz and, sure enough, the harp began to play. The couple spun round the square merrily and were happy enough to give the young man two pennies.

More and more people came by and asked for tunes. The young man rubbed his hands with pleasure. "I shall surely make my fortune now," he said to himself.

Weeks passed and the young man did, indeed, make a lot of money. He didn't care at all how much he charged. If someone who looked wealthy came along he might charge them six pennies or even eight. By now, he had completely forgotten that he had stolen the harp and that it didn't belong to him at all. He bought himself fine clothes and ate expensive food and generally considered himself rather clever.

Then one day, an old man in a broad-brimmed hat came past and asked for a tune. He grumbled a bit when the young man asked for two pennies but held out the coins, making sure the young man could not see his face – for he was the pedlar!

"I'd like the harp to play a tune to drive you mad," said the old man. The young man thought this was a strange request but he had taken the coins and the harp had already started to play.

It played a short and very silly tune. Then, it played it again. And again. And again. And again. It simply wouldn't stop. By now, the old man had slipped away, so when people weren't watching the young man tried to kick the harp, but it side-stepped him and carried on playing. On and on it went, playing that infuriating tune. The young man put his hands over his ears to block out the noise, but the harp just played louder.

Passers-by moved away. "What a terrible tune," they said. The young man tried to move away, too, but the harp just followed him down the road, still playing.

Everywhere he went, night and day, the harp followed the young man until he was at his wits' end. He had used up all his money and he was in despair. Finally, he thought there was only one thing to do. He must go back to the pedlar and beg him to stop the harp. It took him a while to make his way back to the town where the pedlar lived, but sure enough there he was, standing in the market square trying to sell a few old pots and pans to passers-by. He looked very unhappy and the young man felt truly sorry for what he had done.

He approached the pedlar with the harp still playing away behind him. He was about to explain when, to his surprise, the pedlar stopped him and said, "I know all about your plight. I will stop the harp playing its maddening tune on one condition."

"I'll do anything," said the young man.

"You must ask people what tune they would liked played and then you must give them a penny each time."

The young man gratefully agreed and the pedlar told the harp to stop playing. The young man had to work very hard to earn enough money to give people their pennies, but he was willing to do so in return for the pedlar making the harp stop playing that maddening tune!

Goldilocks and the Three Bears

There once lived a little girl who had long, golden hair. Because of this, everyone knew her as Goldilocks. Goldilocks and her mother lived together in a cosy little cottage in the forest.

"Would you like some pretty flowers?" Goldilocks asked her mother one day. "I will pick you some if you like."

"That would be lovely, my dear," said her mother. "But mind you don't get lost. Don't stray too far and don't be too long."

Goldilocks gave her mother a big hug and promised to be careful. She picked up her little flower basket and skipped off into the forest to look for flowers.

First, she came upon some big, bright daffodils. She picked a few and placed them in her basket. A little further on, she spied some pretty bluebells and so she picked a bunch of those as well. Then she saw, even further on, some lovely marigolds, which she also picked and put into her basket.

Well, Goldilocks was so busy picking all these wonderful flowers that she wandered further and further into the forest. Suddenly, she realized that she was lost. She didn't know which way to turn. She was also beginning to feel very hungry and tired.

Just when she was wondering what to do next, she saw a small cottage nestling among the trees. She went up to it and looked through the windows, but couldn't see anyone inside. But the door was open and so she went in. Inside the cottage she found a table laid out with three bowls of steaming porridge. There was a big bowl, a medium-sized bowl and a little bowl. The table also had three chairs arranged around it, one next to each of the bowls of porridge. There was a big chair, a medium-sized chair and a little chair.

Goldilocks was so tired that she simply had to sit down. First, she sat down in the big chair, but it was very hard and lumpy. It wasn't comfortable at all. Then, she tried the medium-sized chair, but that didn't feel comfortable either. At last, she tried the little chair, but as soon as she sat down in it – it broke! She was too heavy for the little chair. "Oh dear," thought Goldilocks.

Instead of sitting down, she thought she would have some porridge, as she was still very hungry. First, she took a spoonful of porridge from the big bowl. But it was too hot and so she couldn't eat it. Then, she tried a spoonful from the medium-sized bowl, but it was too lumpy. So she tried a spoonful from the little bowl. And guess what? It tasted so delicious that she ate it all up!

"Oh, I do feel sleepy," yawned Goldilocks after she had finished the porridge in the little bowl. "I wonder if there is a nice, comfortable bed I can sleep in."

So she went upstairs and found a bedroom with three beds in it. There was a big bed, a medium-sized bed and a little bed. First, she tried the big bed, but it was very hard and didn't feel comfortable at all. Next, she tried the medium-sized bed, but it was too soft and that didn't feel comfortable either. Finally, she tried the little bed. It was just right – warm and cosy. Soon, she was fast asleep.

Just then, the family of three bears who lived in the cottage came back from their walk in the forest. As soon as they came in through the front door, they knew someone had been there.

"Who has been sitting in
my chair?" said Daddy Bear,
in a deep, gruff voice.

"And who has been
sitting in my chair?"
asked Mummy Bear
in a softer voice.

"Who has broken
my chair?" cried Baby
Bear in a squeaky voice.

Then, the three bears looked on the table.

"Someone has been trying my porridge," said Daddy Bear.

"And someone has been trying my porridge, too," said Mummy Bear.

"Who has eaten all my porridge?" said Baby Bear, who by now was very upset and sobbing big tears.

Upstairs went the three bears and into their bedroom.

"Who has been sleeping in my bed?" asked Daddy Bear.

"And who has been sleeping in my bed?" asked Mummy Bear.

Suddenly, Baby Bear gave a cry of surprise. "Look!" he yelled. "There's someone sleeping in my bed."

Goldilocks woke up with a start when she heard all the noise. She looked up to see the three bears staring down at her. She was so frightened that she jumped straight out of bed, down the stairs and out through the front door. Then, she ran and ran until she arrived back home to her own cottage again.

And do you know, that was the last that the three bears ever saw of Goldilocks!

"Whatever shall I do?" wondered the chocolate soldier. "I'm sure to get eaten by a bigger fish or maybe even a shark!" He tried to turn around and swim against the river's flow but it was no good. The current swept him away down river again.

Soon, he could see the waves on the shore. He smelt the sea air and tasted the salt in the water. Now, he found himself bobbing up and down on the sea. He could see a boat not far away and then all of a sudden he felt a net closing around him. He struggled to get out, but the net only tightened and soon he felt himself being hauled out of the water and landed with a "thwack!" on the deck among a pile of fish. The smell was awful and the chocolate soldier was quite relieved when he felt the boat being rowed towards the shore.

"I'll hop over the side as soon as we land and run away," he thought, quite forgetting that he had no legs but only a fish's tail.

But there was no chance of escape. As soon as the boat reached the shore, he and all the other fish were flung into buckets and lifted into a van. The van stopped outside a shop and a man carried the buckets inside, where it smelt of fried fish, chips

and vinegar. The chocolate soldier found himself
being lifted up with a lot of other fish in a huge metal
basket. He looked down and saw a terrible sight below.
They were heading for a vat of boiling oil! At that very
moment, he felt very peculiar once again. His scales melted,
his tail drooped and he felt himself slide through the holes in the
basket and into the pocket of a man's overalls.

    The chocolate soldier lay in the corner of the pocket, while the
man worked all day in the shop. Then, the man headed for home,
with the chocolate soldier bouncing up and down in the overall
pocket as the man walked along. Soon, they arrived at the man's
house. He reached into his pocket.

    "Look what I've found," he said to his small son. "A coin. Here,
you can have it – but don't spend it all at once!" he said, chuckling
to himself. The chocolate soldier felt himself being passed from
one hand to another.

"So now, I've hardened into the shape of a chocolate coin," he thought. "And I'm going to be eaten by the boy!" But to his surprise, he found himself being slipped into the boy's pocket.

The chocolate soldier felt himself bouncing up and down in the child's pocket as he ran up the street and into a shop. The chocolate soldier peeped out and to his astonishment saw that he was back in Mrs Brown's sweet shop. Then, he realized what was happening. The boy believed he was a real coin and was going to try and spend him! The boy stood in the queue at the counter.

The chocolate soldier called out to his soldier friends in the window, "Pssst! It's me! Help me get out of here!" One of the soldiers looked down, but all he could see was a chocolate coin sticking out of the boy's pocket. Then, he recognized the voice.

"I'm a chocolate soldier like you, but I've been turned into a coin. Help!" cried the chocolate soldier.

114

"Leave it to me," replied the soldier on the shelf. "Don't worry, we'll have you out of there in a jiffy!"

The word was passed along and, quick as a flash, one of the sugar mice chewed off a length of liquorice bootlace. Then, the soldier lowered the lace into the boy's pocket, where it stuck to the chocolate coin. Carefully, the soldiers hauled the coin up on to the shelf. The chocolate soldier was delighted to find his foil uniform was still there on the shelf, just where it had been before. All the effort of getting on to the shelf had made him quite warm and he found he could slip quite easily back through the hole in the shoe and into his uniform again.

"I'd like a chocolate soldier," said the boy to Mrs Brown. But when he reached in his pocket the coin had gone.

"Never mind," said kind Mrs Brown, "I'll let you have one anyway." She reached into the window and took down a soldier from the end of the row and gave it to the boy. And as for our chocolate soldier? In the cool of the night, he turned back into a smart-looking soldier again.

Somewhere along the trail he had started following the wrong tail and now he was hopelessly lost. He wanted to cry out for his mother but then he remembered that he was the bravest lion in all of Africa. So what do you think he did? He went straight up to the mother elephant and growled his fiercest growl at her. "That'll frighten her!" thought Lenny. "She won't dare growl back!" And, of course, she didn't growl back. Instead she lifted her trunk and trumpeted so loudly at Lenny that he was blown off his feet and through the air and landed against the hard trunk of a tree.

Lenny got up and found that his knees were knocking. "Oh my," he thought, "that elephant has a very loud growl. But I'm still definitely the bravest lion in all of Africa." He set off across the plain. It was getting hot in the midday Sun and soon Lenny began to feel sleepy. "I think I'll just take a nap in that tree," he thought and started climbing up into the branches.

To his surprise, he found that the tree was already occupied by a large leopard. "I'll show him who's boss," thought Lenny, baring his tiny claws. The leopard raised his head to look at Lenny and then bared his own huge, razor-sharp claws. He took a swipe at Lenny with his paw. Without even touching Lenny, the wind from the leopard's great paw swept Lenny out of the tree and he landed with a bump on the ground.

Lenny got up and found that his legs were trembling. "Oh my," he thought, "that leopard had big claws. But I'm still definitely the bravest lion in Africa." He set off again across the plain. After a while, he began to feel quite hungry. "I wonder what I can find to eat," he thought. Just then, he saw a spotted shape lying low in the grass. "That looks like a tasty meal," thought Lenny, as he pounced on the spotted shape. But the spotted shape was a cheetah!

The Giant Who Shrank

Once upon a time, in a far-off land, there lived a huge giant.
He made his home in a big cave high up in the mountains.
His bed, table and chairs were made from great tree trunks.
And when he wanted a drink, he simply filled an old bathtub
with water and drank it down in one enormous gulp. When he
snored – which he did almost every night – it sounded
like a huge thunderstorm and the
noise echoed all around
the mountains.

At the bottom of the mountains there was a village, but all the people in the village were very different from the giant, for they were not big at all. They were just like you and me. They were afraid of the giant, of course, and whenever he came striding down the mountains to hunt, they all ran away into the woods or locked themselves inside their houses. Sometimes, the clumsy giant would tramp around the village squashing houses with his great feet as he went and that only made the villagers even more frightened of him!

123

Although the giant was so big and strong, he was not a bad giant, but he was very, very lonely because everyone ran away whenever he appeared. Sometimes, while he was sitting alone in his cave, he could hear the villagers having feasts and parties and he longed to join them and be just like them.

One day, when the giant was tramping around the village as usual, something glinting in the Sun caught his eye. At the top of a big tree (which of course was not very big as far as the giant was concerned) lay a gold box.

124

The giant bent down and picked up the box. To his surprise he heard a small voice inside say, "Help! Help! Let me out!"

The giant opened the box and out jumped an elf. "Thank you, thank you, large sir," he said. "I am a magic elf, but one of my spells went wrong and I got locked inside this box. No one in the village could hear me calling for help high up in this tree."

To show his thanks, the elf said he would grant the giant one wish.

"I wish I could be the same as all the other villagers," boomed the giant.

"What a difficult wish," said the elf.

"You are so big! But I will do my best."

The elf closed his eyes and chanted a magic spell. But nothing seemed to happen – the giant was still as big as ever.

The giant was very sad to
discover that he had not shrunk,
but he wished the elf well, thanked
him for trying and went on his way.
As the giant was walking back to his
cave in the mountains, he noticed
something strange. All the puddles
of water that he had passed on the
way down to the village had got
bigger. They were as big as lakes
now! The giant looked up to see if
it had been raining, but the sky was
clear and blue.

Then, another strange thing
happened. The big stone steps
he had cut in the mountainside
leading up to his cave had also
got bigger! He could hardly
clamber up them.

Eventually, puffing and panting,
the giant reached the door to his
cave. But he could not reach the
doorknob. It now towered
above him, far from his reach.

126

"What is happening?" thought the giant. "The elf's spell must have gone wrong. Not only am I still a giant, but everything around me has now got even bigger."

Suddenly, the truth came to him. Of course! Everything had not become bigger – he had become smaller! The spell had worked after all. Now he was just the same as the other people in the village.

He made his way to the village, wondering if everyone would still run away as before. But he need not have worried. All the villagers welcomed him into the village and he lived there happily among them for the rest of his days.

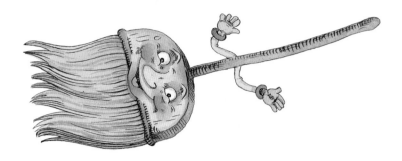

The Naughty Broom

"Goodness me, what a lot of dirt and dust there is all over this kitchen floor," said the maid. She was a very house-proud maid and didn't like dirt and dust on her floor one little bit. Out came the broom from its place in the cupboard in the corner and soon the maid was busily sweeping the floor and brushing all the dirt and dust into a big dustpan.

Unfortunately, this kitchen also had elves living in it. They were too tiny to see, of course, but if you upset them they could be very mischievous indeed. As the broom worked away, it swept into one dark corner where the elves were having a party. Suddenly, the King elf was swept away from their little table and into the dustpan! The next thing he knew he was being thrown, with all the other rubbish, on to the rubbish tip.

Coughing and spluttering with rage, the King elf finally climbed out from under all the rubbish in the rubbish tip and stood on top of it. He picked the dirt and dust out of his ears and nose, pulled a fish bone from out of his trousers and tried to look as king-like as he could, having just been thrown on to a rubbish tip. "Who did this?" he squeaked at the top of his voice. "I'll make someone very, very sorry indeed," he vowed.

Eventually, he made his way back to the house and into the kitchen again. The other elves looked at the King elf and did their best not to laugh. For the King elf was still looking very dirty and untidy and still had bits of rubbish stuck all over him. But the other elves knew better than to laugh at the King, because he was likely to cast a bad spell on them if they did.

"It was the broom that did it," chorused all the other elves.

"Right," said the King elf, "then I'm going to cast a bad spell on the broom."

The broom was by now back in its cupboard. The King elf marched over to the cupboard and jumped in through the keyhole. The King elf pointed to the broom and said,

"Bubble, bubble, gubble, gubble,

Go and cause a lot of trouble!"

And with that the broom suddenly stood to attention, its bristles quivering. It was night time now and everyone in the house was asleep. The broom opened its cupboard door and sprang into the kitchen. It then unlocked the kitchen door and went outside. Straight to the rubbish tip it went, and with a flick of its bristles, swept a huge pile of rubbish back into the kitchen. Tin cans, dirt, dust, chicken bones and goodness knows what else all got swept on to the kitchen floor. The broom then closed the kitchen door, took itself back to its cupboard and all was quiet until morning.

130

When the maid came down into the kitchen, she couldn't believe her eyes. "Who has made this awful mess?" she said. "If I find out it was those cats ..." she threatened. She took the broom from the cupboard and swept all the rubbish back outside again.

The next night, the same thing happened. Once it was quiet and everyone in the house was asleep, out of its cupboard came the broom, and into the house came all the rubbish again, swept there as before by the naughty broom. This time, there were fish heads, old bottles and all the soot from the fireplaces.

Well, the maid was speechless. After clearing up again, she got the gardener to burn all the rubbish from the rubbish tip, so that nothing else could be brought in – although she still had no idea how it had happened.

131

That very night, the naughty broom decided it would make a
mess in a different way. So instead of sweeping in rubbish from
outside, the broom flew up to the shelves and knocked all the
jars to the ground. With a crash they fell to the floor, one after
another, and spread their contents everywhere.

"Stop this AT ONCE!" demanded a voice suddenly.

The broom stopped its mischief.

"What do you think you are doing?" said the voice again. The
voice had come from a very stern-looking fairy who was now
standing on the draining board, with her hands on her hips.
What the broom did not know was that one of the bottles it had
knocked down contained a good fairy, imprisoned by the elves.
Now she was at last free, the spell was broken and it was her turn
to cast a spell.

THE NAUGHTY BROOM

"Broom, broom, sweep this floor,
Make it cleaner than ever before.
Find the elves that cast your spell,
And sweep them off into the well," she chanted.

The broom went to work. It seemed to sweep so fast that its
bristles just became a blur. Into this corner it went, then into that
and into every nook and cranny it swept. Every bit of dirt and
dust, and all the broken bottles, were swept into the dustpan and
then out of the house. Then, it came back and swept all the elves
down into the well where they couldn't do any more mischief.

In the morning, the maid came down to find a spotlessly clean
kitchen. She was puzzled to find some of the jars missing, but
between you and me she was also rather pleased. It just meant
that there were fewer things to dust.

The Sad Clown

Bongo the clown had a bit of a problem. Clowns were supposed to be happy, funny, jolly people, but Bongo was a very sad clown. Nothing at all seemed to make him laugh.

Whenever the circus came to town people from all around flocked to the big top hoping for an exciting day out. They thrilled to the daring performance of the high-wire act, as the acrobats leaped from one swinging trapeze to the next. They enjoyed the jugglers, who tossed bright, sparkling balls into the air while standing on one leg. And the crowd delighted in seeing the beautiful white horses parading around the circus ring with the bareback riders balancing on their backs. When the seals came on, there was always a big cheer from the crowd, for everyone loved them and could watch their clever antics for hours.

But the biggest favourite of the crowd, especially with all
the children, was the clown. Dressed in his big baggy trousers
he would enter the circus ring with his funny walk. Everyone
laughed to see him. They laughed even more when they saw his
big floppy hat with the revolving flower on it. Even his painted
clown face made them laugh.

But when his act started, the crowd thought they would burst
with laughter. First of all, his bicycle fell apart as he tried to ride
around the ring. Then, he fell out of his motor car when the seat
tipped up. By the time he had accidentally poured cold water
down his trousers and fallen into the custard-filled swimming
pool, the crowd were almost crying with laughter.

But beneath all the makeup, Bongo the sad clown wasn't smiling at all. In fact, he saw nothing funny at all in bicycles that fell apart as you used them, or cars that tipped you out as you went along, or having cold water poured down your trousers, or even ending up face first in a swimming pool full of custard. He simply hadn't got a sense of humour.

All the other performers in the circus decided they would try and cheer the sad clown up.

"I know," said the high-wire trapeze acrobat, "let's paint an even funnier face on him. That'll make him laugh."

So that's what they did, but Bongo still didn't laugh and was still just as sad.

"Let us perform some of our tricks, just for him," said the seals.

So they sat on their stools and tossed their big coloured balls to each other, clapped their flippers together and made lots of honking sounds. But Bongo still didn't laugh. In fact, nothing that anyone tried made poor Bongo smile. He was still a very sad clown.

Then, Percival the ringmaster spoke. "You know, I think I know what the problem is," he said. "There is nothing a clown likes better than playing tricks on other clowns. Perhaps if we had a second clown, that would cheer Bongo up."

So right away they hired another clown, called Piffle.

The circus arrived in the next town and soon it was time for
Bongo and Piffle's act. Piffle started riding around on his bike
while Bongo pretended to wash the car by throwing a bucket of
water over it. Instead of the water landing on the car, of course, it
went all over Piffle, who just happened to be cycling past at that
moment. A little smile flickered across Bongo's face at the sight of
the soaking wet Piffle.

Next, Bongo and Piffle pretended to be cooking and Bongo
tripped while carrying two huge custard pies. Both landed right
in Piffle's face. Bongo let out a huge chuckle of laughter when he
saw Piffle's custard-covered face.

THE SAD CLOWN

At the end of their act, the clowns were pretending to be decorators, painting up a ladder. Of course, you've guessed it. The ladders fell down and all the pots of paint landed on the two clowns. Bongo looked across at Piffle, who had a big paint pot stuck on his head, with paint dripping down his body. Bongo threw back his head and roared with laughter. Piffle thought Bongo looked just as funny with paint all over his body, too. And as for the crowd – well, they thought two clowns were even funnier than one and they clapped and cheered and filled the big top with laughter. After that Bongo was never a sad clown again.

Snow White

In the middle of winter, a young queen sat sewing by an open window. As she looked up and saw the snow falling, she pricked her finger and three drops of blood fell on to the snow. The red of the blood on the white snow, framed by the black ebony window frame, was so striking that the Queen made a wish that she could have a child that was as red as blood, as white as snow and as black as ebony.

In time, the Queen's wish came true. She gave birth to a baby girl with snow-white skin, blood-red lips and hair as black as ebony. The young Queen died soon after the child was born and the King named his daughter, Snow White. Soon, the King took a second wife, as beautiful as the first. But this one was also vain. She had a magic mirror and sometimes she stood in front of it and said, "Mirror, mirror, on the wall, who is the fairest of them all?"

And the mirror answered, "You are the fairest one of all."

Then, the Queen was happy because she knew that the mirror always told the truth.

Years passed and Snow White grew more and more beautiful. One day, the Queen stood in front of the mirror and asked, "Mirror, mirror, on the wall, who is the fairest of them all?"

And the mirror answered, "You were the fairest one, 'tis true, but now Snow White is lovelier than you."

From that moment on, the Queen began to hate Snow White. She couldn't rest until she was rid of the girl, so she called her huntsman and said, "Take Snow White into the forest and kill her. And bring back her heart."

The huntsman could not bear to kill the little girl. He told Snow White to run away into the woods. "She won't survive for long without food and shelter," thought the huntsman with remorse. To satisfy the Queen, he shot a wild boar and took back its heart.

Snow White went deeper into the woods until she was
completely lost. At last, she came to a house. Inside was a table
with a white cloth laid for seven people, with food and drink at
every place. Along one wall were seven beds covered with white
duvets. Snow White was so hungry that she took a mouthful
from each plate and a sip from each cup. Then, she tried out
all the beds but they were all too long, or too short, or too wide
or too narrow – until she came to the last one of all, which was
just right. She lay down and fell fast asleep. Some time later, the
owners of the house returned. They were seven dwarfs who
worked all day mining gold in the mountains. They could soon
tell that they had received a visitor.

"Someone's been sitting in my chair,"
said the first dwarf.

"And eating my food," said the second.

"And drinking my wine," said the third.

"And using my knife," said the fourth.

"And my fork," said the fifth.

"And my spoon," said the sixth.

"And she's asleep on my bed!" said the seventh dwarf.

The dwarfs all crowded around Snow White. She looked so comfortable that they let her sleep in peace.

In the morning, when Snow White woke up, she was frightened at first, but the dwarfs reassured her. She told them what had happened. "You can stay with us," they said. "You can clean our house, cook and wash for us and we will protect you." So Snow White stayed with the dwarfs. Each day, when they went off to work they reminded her, "Don't let anyone in." And Snow White promised that she wouldn't.

For a while the Queen felt happy again now that she thought Snow White was dead. Then one day, she stood in front of the mirror again and asked, "Mirror, mirror, on the wall, who is the fairest of them all?"

And the mirror answered, "Over the hills where the seven dwarfs dwell, Snow White is still alive and well. And though you are fairer than most, 'tis true, she is still far lovelier than you."

The Queen was furious. "This time I'll finish her off myself," she screeched. Disguising herself as a pedlar she made the journey to the dwarfs' house. "Silks for sale. Ribbons and laces," she called.

Snow White looked out of the window and saw the fine things. "Surely it wouldn't hurt to look," she thought. She unlocked the door and chose a pretty lace.

"Let me thread it for you," offered the old woman. Then, she laced Snow White's bodice so tightly that the girl couldn't breathe and she fell to the floor unconscious.

When the dwarfs returned that night, they found her and cut the laces. Snow White began to breathe again and soon she was able to tell them what had happened. "That was the Queen," they told her, "and she'll be back."

For a while all was well, then again the Queen stood in front of her mirror and asked, "Mirror, mirror, on the wall, who is the fairest of them all?"

And again the mirror answered, "Over the hills where the seven dwarfs dwell, Snow White is still alive and well. And though you are fairer than most, 'tis true, she is still far lovelier than you."

The Queen was furious. This time she prepared a poisoned comb and set off for the dwarfs' house in a different disguise. "Come and buy my lovely combs," she called. This time Snow White refused to open the door. "Let me pass you one through the window," said the Queen.

"Well there's no harm in that," thought Snow White, undoing the latch.

The Queen leaned through the window. "Let me comb your lovely hair with this fine comb," she said. As soon as the comb touched Snow White's head, the poison began to work and she fell senseless to the ground.

The dwarfs came home to find Snow White lying on the floor. Carefully, they removed the comb and she returned to life. Meanwhile, the Queen returned to the castle and immediately went up to the mirror and repeated her question. Imagine her anger when she got the same reply as before. Now, she prepared a special apple. One side was green, while the other was red. The Queen poisoned the red half, then she set off for the dwarfs' house once more. This time she pretended to be a farmer's wife. Once again, Snow White refused to open the door. "Don't worry," said the Queen. "Have an apple anyway." She held out the poisoned apple.

"No, no, I mustn't," said Snow White, though the apple did look very tasty.

"Tell you what," said the Queen, "we'll have half each."

"Well, it can't be poisoned," thought Snow White.

The Queen carefully cut the apple in half. "Here, I'll have the sour green half and you have the nice sweet red half," she said. Snow White took the apple, but the moment she bit into it she fell down dead.

The Queen hurried back to the castle and this time when she spoke to the mirror it replied, to her pleasure, "You are the fairest one of all."

The dwarfs came home and found Snow White. They wept bitterly when they saw that she was dead. They placed her in a glass coffin and set it on a hillside and took turns to guard her. One day, a prince came upon the coffin. He was so moved by Snow White that he asked the dwarfs if he could take her with him. He was heartbroken when the dwarfs refused. In the end, they took pity upon him and agreed. As the prince's servants lifted the coffin, one of them stumbled. The apple dislodged itself from her throat and Snow White came back to life.

The Prince asked Snow White to marry him and when she agreed, everyone was invited to the wedding and nothing more was ever heard of the wicked Queen.

The Magic Tree

Tommy rubbed his eyes, blinked hard and looked out of his bedroom window again. But it was still there – an enormous oak tree that definitely hadn't been there yesterday! If it had been there, he'd have known all about it for sure. For a start he would have climbed up it, for Tommy loved nothing better than climbing trees.

No, this tree was definitely not there yesterday! Tommy sat staring at the tree in wonder and disbelief. The tree stood there, outside his bedroom window, with its huge, spreading branches almost asking to be climbed. Tommy wondered how on earth it had suddenly got there, but he decided that before he wondered about that too much, he had better go and climb it first. After all, there was always time later to wonder about things but never enough time to do things, he thought.

As soon as he was dressed, he ran outside to take a closer look at the new tree. It seemed just like any other big oak tree. It had lots of wide, inviting branches and lots of green, rounded leaves. And it had deep, furrowed bark just like any other oak tree.

Tommy couldn't resist any longer. On to the lowest branch he stepped and then up to the next. The tree seemed so easy to climb. There were branches everywhere. In no time at all, he was in a green, leafy canopy. He couldn't even see the ground any more. But something seemed not quite right. The branches beneath his feet seemed to be so big now that he could stand up on them and walk in any direction. And the branches all around him seemed just like trees themselves. In fact, he suddenly realized that he wasn't any longer climbing a tree, but standing in a whole forest full of trees.

Tommy didn't like this at all and thought he had better get down. But where was down? All he could see were tall, swaying trees and here and there a twisty path leading off even deeper into the forest. Tommy didn't know how he had done it, but he had somehow got himself completely lost in a forest and he hadn't even had breakfast yet!

Worse still, it seemed to be getting dark. "Quick, over here!" a voice suddenly called out. Tommy was very startled, but he was even more startled when he saw that the voice belonged to a squirrel.

"You can speak!" blurted out Tommy.

"Of course I can speak!" snapped the squirrel. "Now listen. You are in great danger and there's no time to lose if we are to save you from the clutches of the evil Wizard of the Woods."

The squirrel quickly explained that, long ago, a spell had been cast on the forest and it had become enchanted. Every now and again, the Wizard of the Woods, who ruled the forest, lured an unsuspecting person into his realm by making a tree appear. Once you climbed the tree, you entered the forest. Escape was almost impossible.

"But why does the Wizard of the Woods want to lure people into the forest?" asked Tommy, rather hoping that he didn't have to hear the answer.

"To turn them into fertilizer to make the trees grow," said the squirrel.

Tommy didn't really know what fertilizer was, but it sounded rather nasty. He was pleased when the squirrel suddenly said, "There is just one way to get you out of here. But we must hurry. Soon it will be dark and the Wizard of the Woods will awake. Once he awakes, he will smell your blood and he will capture you."

151

With that, the squirrel jumped up the nearest tree. "Follow me," he said.

Tommy immediately climbed after the squirrel. "Where are we going?" he panted, as they climbed higher and higher.

"To the top of the tallest tree in the forest," the squirrel answered as they clambered from tree to tree, climbing ever higher.

"But why?" asked Tommy.

"Because that's the only way to escape. You'll see!" said the squirrel.

Eventually, they stopped climbing. They were at the top of the tallest tree in the forest. Below them and around them was nothing but more trees. Tommy looked up and at last he could see the clear, twilight sky. He also noticed something rather strange. All the leaves at the top of the tallest tree were enormous.

"Quick, time is running out," said the squirrel. "Sit on this leaf and hold tight."

Tommy sat on one of the huge leaves. The squirrel whistled and before Tommy could blink he had been joined by a hundred more squirrels. They each took hold of the branch to which the leaf was attached. With a great heave, they pulled and pulled until the branch was bent backwards. Suddenly, they let go. With a mighty "TWANG", the branch, with Tommy and the leaf attached, sprang forward. As it did so, Tommy and the leaf were launched into the air. High above the trees they soared until, ever so slowly, they began to float down to Earth. Down, down, they went, until they landed with a bump.

Tommy opened his eyes to find himself on his bedroom floor. He ran over to the window and looked out. The magic tree was nowhere to be seen. It had gone as quickly as it had appeared. But perhaps it had never been there at all. Maybe it was just a dream. What do you think?

The Bee Who Wanted More Stripes

Bertie the bee was a rather vain young bee. Every morning, as soon as he woke up, he would find a large dewdrop in which to admire his reflection. The thing that Bertie liked best about himself was his stripes. He thought stripes were the smartest, flashiest fashion accessory any animal could have. He just wished he had more stripes. But he only had a couple. "Still," he thought, "they are very fine stripes."

Then, he had an idea. What if he could get some more stripes? He would be the stripiest bee around and then everyone else would admire him, too. "I know what I'll do," he said. "I'll ask some other very stripy animals how they got all their stripes and maybe I can copy them."

He buzzed off through the wood, looking for striped animals to ask. He flew across the fields and then the sea and at last he reached a place where there seemed to be quite a few striped animals. The first animal he approached looked like a striped horse. "Hello, horsey!" said Bertie, landing on the beast's nose.

"I'm not a horse – I'm a zebra. And get off my nose!" said the zebra crossly.

"I do beg your pardon," said Bertie. "I just wanted to ask you how you got your stripes."

"Well," said the zebra, "I used to be all brown. Then one day, I came across a piano in the middle of the plain. As I walked past the piano, its black and white keys started to play a tune all by themselves. Then, I looked down and found I had turned black and white, too. And if you believe that you'll believe anything!" And with that the zebra laughed and trotted off.

Bertie continued on his way. Now, he could see a large striped cat. "Hello, puss!" said Bertie, landing on the creature's back.

"I'm not a cat – I'm a tiger. And get off my back!" growled the tiger.

"I'm so sorry," said Bertie, "I just wanted to ask you how you got your stripes."

"Well," said the tiger, "I used to be all yellow. Then one day, when I was a cub, I was playing with a ball of black string and I got all tangled up in it. And that's how I got my stripes. And if you believe that you'll believe anything!"
And the tiger started to laugh
as he stalked off.

Bertie continued on his way. Soon, he could see a long striped worm slithering through the grass. "Hello, little worm!" called Bertie, landing on the worm's tail.

"I'm not a worm – I'm a snake. And get off my tail!" hissed the snake.

"Oh dear. I didn't mean to upset you," said Bertie. "I just wanted to ask you how you got your stripes."

"Well," said the snake, "I used to be all brown. Then one day, I was crossing a road just as the traffic lights were changing from red to green and when I reached the other side I found that I was striped red and green from head to tail. And if you believe that you'll believe anything!" And the snake started to laugh as he slithered away.

Bertie continued on his way once more. Then, he spotted a squirrel with a striped tail in a tree. "Hello, squirrel!" he said, landing on the animal's paw.

"I'm not a squirrel – I'm a ring-tailed lemur. And get off my paw!" said the ring-tailed lemur angrily.

"I do apologize," said Bertie. "I just wanted to ask you how you got your striped tail."

"Well," said the ring-tailed lemur, "my tail used to be all white. Then one day, I was playing hoop-la with my friends. I said they could use my tail as a target and so they threw all the rings on to my tail. But they got stuck. And that's how I got a striped tail. And if you believe that you'll believe anything!" And the ring-tailed lemur started to laugh as he scampered away.

"Well," thought Bertie, "I'd better give it a go!" First, he looked for a piano on the plain, but to no avail. There just wasn't a piano to be found. Then, he looked for a ball of string – but he couldn't find one of those, either. He did find a set of traffic lights and he buzzed backwards and forwards in front of them until he felt quite dizzy, but he still had the same number of stripes. Finally, he called out, "Anyone fancy a game of hoop-la?" But there was no reply. It was night time and all the animals were asleep.

"I'll just have to make my way home," thought Bertie sadly. He flew all through the night and arrived home exhausted in the morning.

Just then, he met Clarice, the wise old bee. "Clarice," said Bertie, "I really would like some more stripes, but although I've asked lots of stripy animals how they got their stripes, all they gave me were silly answers."

Clarice looked at Bertie rather sternly and said, "You only get the stripes you were born with, Bertie. And besides, do you know what you would be if you had more stripes? You would be a wasp!"

Bertie looked horrified. The last thing he wanted to be was a wasp. Wasps were always going around frightening and stinging everyone and no one liked them at all.

Bertie thought for a few moments and then said, "Perhaps having just a few stripes but being liked by others is better after all."

The Invisible Imp

One day, Sarah Jones was pegging out her washing. It was a lovely day and she was looking forward to visiting her friend Rose. "I'll just get this washing on the line while the Sun's shining," she said to herself, "and then I'll be on my way."

After a while, she stopped and looked down into the basket. "That's very peculiar!" she thought. "I know I've already pegged out that green shirt and there it is back in the basket." She carried on pegging out the clothes. Now, she shook her head in disbelief. For although she had been working away for quite a while, the basket of washing was still full and there was almost nothing on the line! She began to get quite cross, for she was going to be late getting to Rose's house.

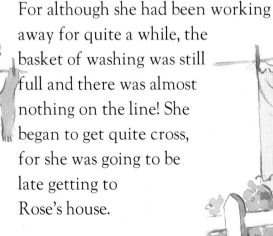

Try as she might, she just could not get that washing pegged. In the end, she had to leave the basket of wet washing and run to Rose's house.

"I'm so sorry I'm late, Rose," she gasped, all out of breath from running. Sarah told Rose all about what had happened.

"Well," said Rose, "that's a strange coincidence. I was baking some cakes for us to have for tea. Every time I put them in the oven and turned away, they were out of the oven and on the table again! In the end I had to stand guard over them – which reminds me, they were just beginning to cook nicely when you knocked on the door."

The two women went into Rose's kitchen and there were the cakes, sitting on the table again, half-cooked. "Now they're ruined!" cried Rose. "Whatever shall we do?"

At that moment, there was a noise in the street. Rose and Sarah looked out of the window to see Elmer, the postman, surrounded by a crowd of people all shouting and waving envelopes in the air. The two women ran out into the street. "What's going on?" they cried.

"Elmer's given us all the wrong post," said Rose's neighbour, Dora. "He's normally so reliable, but this morning he seems to have gone completely crazy. Now we've got to sort out all the post for him."

"I don't know what's happened," wailed Elmer in anguish. "I'm sure I posted all the letters through the right doors."

"Well," said Sarah, "Rose and I have also found strange things happening to us this morning." She told the crowd their stories. Everyone forgave Elmer when they realized it wasn't his fault, but they were still truly mystified as to what – or who – could have caused all these problems.

But that wasn't the end of it. Oh no, indeed! The butcher's wife served her family mutton stew, but when she lifted the lid the family heard a bleating sound and a little lamb leaped out of the pot. The milkman delivered the milk as usual, but when people took their milk indoors, they found the bottles were full of lemonade. Old Mr Smith tried to pull his chair up to the table and found it was stuck hard to the floor. And when Mrs Smith painted her bedroom blue, she came back and found it had changed to pink with purple spots.

Can you guess what had happened? Do you know who'd been up to all these tricks? It was an imp, of course! The wicked little fellow had become bored playing pranks on the fairies and goblins in fairyland. By now, they knew all his tricks and he was finding it harder and harder to catch them out. Then, he had an idea. Why not play tricks in the human world where he would be invisible? So that's exactly what he did.

At first, he really only
meant to play one or two
tricks, but he had such
fun that he couldn't resist
carrying on.

Well, the invisible imp
continued on with his tricks. But of
course, as you know, pride comes before a fall and
one day he just went too far. Sarah Jones had been
invited to a party. It was to be a fancy dress party and
on the invitation it said: "*Please wear red*". Now, Sarah
fretted because she had no red clothes at all. Then, she
had an idea. She got out an old blue dress from the back
of the cupboard. "I'll dye it red," she thought.

She mixed a big bucket of red dye and was just about to put
the dress into it, when along came the invisible imp. "Here's
some fun!" he thought. "I'll turn the dye blue. Then she won't
know why her dress hasn't changed colour. Won't that be
funny!" And he started giggling to himself
at the thought of it. He danced up and
down on the edge of the bucket,
thinking up a really evil spell
to turn the dye blue. But he
laughed so much to himself that
he slipped and fell right into the
bright red mixture. Fast as lightning

164

out he scrambled and cast his spell.

Sure enough Sarah fished out the dress from the bucket and to her dismay saw that it was exactly the same colour as when she had put it into the dye. She was about to peer into the bucket when something caught her eye. For there, sitting on the table, chuckling to himself and holding his sides with laughter, was a bright red imp. And there was a trail of tiny red footprints from the bucket of dye to the table. The silly imp had no idea that he was no longer invisible and that Sarah could see him as plain as the nose on her face! In a flash Sarah realized what had happened. She chased the imp out of the house and down the street and, I'm glad to say, he wasn't able to play his mischievous tricks ever again.

Ursula's Umbrella

Ursula was a little girl who longed for adventure. She loved reading stories about far-away places and explorers and even children like herself who had amazing adventures. "Why doesn't anything interesting ever happen to me?" she sighed. "How I wish I could fly to the Moon or dive to the deepest part of the ocean. What fun it would be!"

One windy day, Ursula went out for a walk. She took her umbrella with her because it looked as though it might be going to rain. Ursula's umbrella was red with a shiny black handle. It was also very large indeed. People used to laugh as Ursula walked along the street with her umbrella up. It looked so big and Ursula was so small that it seemed as though the umbrella was walking along all by itself!

As Ursula walked up the street she felt a few raindrops on her nose. "Better put up my umbrella," she thought. She unfurled her umbrella and lifted it up above her head. As she did so, a great gust of wind came and swept her right off the pavement. It carried her past the upstairs windows of the houses, past the roofs and the chimney pots and up, up, into the sky. Ursula clung tightly to the umbrella handle. She was surprised to find she didn't feel the least bit frightened. No, not a bit. She felt very excited. She looked down and saw streets and factories whizzing past far below. Then, she saw fields and something that looked like a silver thread snaking through the countryside. "A river!" thought Ursula.

Now, she could see the coastline and soon the umbrella was carrying her out over the ocean. At first when she looked down the sea was grey, but gradually it turned to the deepest blue with frothy white waves. "How I'd love a swim," thought Ursula. At that moment, she felt the umbrella starting to descend. Looking down she could see that they were heading for an island in the middle of the ocean. Soon, she was floating past the tops of palm trees and, as she touched the ground, she felt sand under her feet.

"I'm going for a swim!" said Ursula to herself. She folded up her umbrella and set off to the beach. The water felt deliciously warm as Ursula paddled about. She looked down and saw that the water was amazingly clear. She could see brightly coloured fish darting in and out of the coral. "Wow!" exclaimed Ursula out loud and then "Wow!" again, though this time much louder as she looked up and saw a black fin skimming through the water towards her. "Shark!" she shrieked, but no one heard.

Then, all of a sudden, a gust of wind made her umbrella unfurl itself and float towards her in the water, like a boat. Ursula made a dash for the umbrella, hurled herself into it and floated away across the sea. "That was quite an adventure!" she thought.

After a while, Ursula looked out over the rim of the umbrella
and saw that it was heading for the shore again. This time, when
Ursula stepped out of the umbrella, she found that she was at
the edge of a jungle. Folding up the umbrella, she set off into
the forest. She followed an overgrown path through the trees. "I
wonder where this leads?" thought Ursula. She wiped her brow
and swatted the insects that flew in front of her face. Deeper and
deeper into the jungle she went.

Suddenly, she heard the sound of rushing water and found
herself standing on the banks of a river. All at once she heard
another sound. It was the crashing noise of some enormous beast
approaching through the trees.

Where could she run to? Suddenly, she felt the umbrella being blown from her hand. To her amazement it fell to the ground, stretching right across the river like a bridge. Ursula walked over to the other side, not daring to look down at the torrent below. When she was safely on the far bank she looked back to see a large mountain lion, with glittering green eyes, glaring at her from the opposite bank. "That was a lucky escape!" thought Ursula.

Ursula could see a mountain through the trees and decided to head towards it. "I'll be able to get a good view from the top and maybe find my way home," she thought. She struggled on through the forest and eventually found herself at the foot of the mountain. There seemed to be no way up the sheer rock face. Ursula was at the point of despair when suddenly, another great gust of wind blew up. It carried Ursula, clinging to her opened umbrella, all the way up to the top of the mountain.

170

At the top of the mountain, the umbrella let her gently down again and her feet landed in deep snow. By now, it was blowing a blizzard and she could not see anything except white snowflakes in all directions. "There's only one thing to do," thought Ursula. She put the umbrella on the snow, sat on it and whizzed all the way down the other side of the mountain.

When she reached the bottom, to her surprise, the umbrella sledge didn't stop but carried on through the snowstorm until eventually, after a very long time, it came to a halt right outside her own front door. "Well, that was quite an adventure," said Ursula, shaking the snow off the umbrella, before folding it up.

She stepped inside the front door. "Wherever have you been?" said her mother. "You look as though you've been to the ends of the Earth and back."

"Well I have," Ursula was about to say. But then, she thought that no one would believe her and it was nicer to keep her adventures to herself. And that is what she did.

Rapunzel

There once lived a man and his wife who had long wished for a child. At last, their wish was granted and the wife found that she was expecting a baby. At the back of their house was a garden that was filled with the most beautiful flowers and herbs. However, the man and his wife did not dare enter the garden, for it was owned by a wicked witch, of whom everyone was scared.

One day, when the woman was standing by her window looking down into the garden, she saw a flower bed full of the prettiest Rapunzel plants she had ever seen. They looked so fresh and green that she felt a great craving to eat some of them. Day after day she would sit by her window, staring at the Rapunzel plants for hours on end. Eventually, she became quite pale and miserable.

"What's wrong, my dear?" said her husband.

"I must have some of that Rapunzel," she replied, "or I may die."

The poor husband decided that the only thing to do was to steal into the witch's garden at night and take some of the plants. Late one night, the man climbed the high wall that surrounded the garden and hastily snatched a bunch of Rapunzel plants and made off with them.

His wife was delighted. She made a salad of them that was so delicious that the next day she said to her husband, "I must have more of that delicious Rapunzel."

So that night, the husband stole once more into the witch's garden. Imagine his horror when he dropped on to the grass to find the witch there lying in wait for him. "How dare you come into my garden and steal my Rapunzel plants," she shrieked. "You'll live to regret this."

173

"Please have mercy on me," begged the man. "I'm not really a thief. I came to help my wife, who is expecting our first child. She told me she would die if she didn't have some of your Rapunzel to eat."

Then, the witch changed her tune. "By all means," she said, "take as much as you like. But in exchange you must give me the baby when it is born. Don't worry – I will care for it as if I were its mother. What do you say?" The man was so terrified that he hastily agreed to what the witch had said. When his wife gave birth to a baby girl the witch immediately appeared to take the child. The witch named her Rapunzel, after the plants that had caused all the trouble, and took the child away with her.

Rapunzel grew very beautiful, strong and healthy, with long golden hair that fell past her waist. When she was twelve years old the witch locked her away at the top of a tower in the middle of a forest. The tower had neither stairs nor a door, but only one window at the top so that nobody but the witch could reach her.

Each day, when the witch visited her, she would stand below the girl's window and call out, "Rapunzel, Rapunzel, let down your hair, that I may climb without a stair."

Then, the girl would wind her long tresses around the window hook and lower her hair all the way to the ground. The witch would climb up it as if it were a ladder. In this way, Rapunzel's lonely life went on for several years.

One day, a young prince was riding in the forest when he heard a sweet voice. It was Rapunzel singing to herself. The Prince was so entranced that he followed the sound and came upon the tower.

But when he could find no way in he became discouraged and rode home. Rapunzel's lovely voice had stirred his heart so deeply, however, that he returned day after day to hear her singing.

One day, as he stood behind a tree, he saw the witch appear and heard her calling, "Rapunzel, Rapunzel, let down your hair, that I may climb without a stair."

Then, he saw a mass of golden hair tumble down and watched the witch climb up it to the window. "Is that the way up?" thought the Prince. "Then I will climb the golden ladder, too."

The next day, around dusk, the Prince went to the tower and called, "Rapunzel, Rapunzel, let down your hair, that I may climb without a stair."

Immediately, the tresses fell down and the Prince climbed up. At first sight of the Prince, Rapunzel was afraid, but the Prince addressed her in such a friendly way that she knew she could trust him. "Once I had heard your voice," said the Prince, "I couldn't rest until I saw you. Now I cannot rest until you agree to marry me."

Rapunzel by now had fallen truly in love with the young man, so she willingly accepted. "I wish I could come away with you," said Rapunzel. "You must bring some silk with you each time you visit and I shall weave a ladder of silk and then I will be able to escape."

Each day, the witch visited Rapunzel and each night the Prince came. The witch suspected nothing until one day Rapunzel forgot herself and said to the witch, "Why are you so much heavier to pull up than the Prince?"

"Oh, treacherous girl!" screamed the witch. "You have deceived me!" She snatched up a pair of scissors and cut off all Rapunzel's lovely hair. Then, the witch drove Rapunzel from the tower and left her in a wild and desolate place to fend for herself as best she could.

That night, along came the Prince to the tower and said, as usual, "Rapunzel, Rapunzel, let down your hair, that I may climb without a stair."

But the witch was lying in wait. She tied Rapunzel's hair to the window hook and let the golden tresses fall to the ground. Up climbed the Prince full of joy, as always. But when he stepped in through the window, it was not his beautiful Rapunzel that met his gaze but the icy glare of the witch. "Aha!" cried the witch with a sneer. "So you thought you could steal my girl, did you? Well she's gone and you'll never set eyes on her again."

Beside himself with grief, the Prince threw himself from the tower and would have died had he not landed in the thickest thorn bushes. Although he survived, the thorns pierced his eyes and blinded him. For many years he wandered through the wilderness grieving for his lost Rapunzel and living on whatever he could find to eat. Eventually, he wandered into the same part of the wilderness where Rapunzel lived with the twins she had borne.

Just as he had done so many years ago, the Prince heard a sweet voice coming through the trees. He made his way towards the sound of the voice. Suddenly, Rapunzel saw him and straight away she recognized him. She ran to him and threw her arms around him weeping. As she wept tears of joy and sorrow, two teardrops fell into his eyes, healing them and restoring his sight.

Then, the two were united again and the Prince took Rapunzel and their children back to his own kingdom and they all lived happily ever after.

Buried Treasure

Jim lived in a big old house with a big rambling garden. The house was rather spooky and Jim much preferred the garden. He would spend hours kicking a football around the overgrown lawn, climbing the old apple trees in the orchard or just staring into the pond in case he might spot a fish. It was a wonderful garden to play in but Jim was not really a happy child because he was lonely. How he wished he had someone to play with! It would be such fun to play football with a friend, or have someone to go fishing with. He had plenty of friends at school, but it was a long bus journey to his home and besides, his school friends found his house so spooky that they only came to visit once.

One day, Jim was hunting about in the garden with a stick. He hoped he might find some interesting small creatures to examine. Every time he found a new creature he would draw it and try to find out its name. So far, he had discovered eight types of snail and six different ladybirds. As he was poking about under some leaves he saw a piece of metal sticking out of the ground. He reached down and pulled it free. In his hand lay a rusty old key. It was quite big and as Jim brushed away the soil, he saw that it was carved with beautiful patterns.

Jim carried the key indoors, where he cleaned and polished it. Then, he set about trying to find the lock that it fitted. First, he tried the old garden gate that had been locked as long as Jim could remember. But the key was far too small. Next, he tried the grandfather clock in the hall. But the key did not fit the clock's lock. Then, he remembered an old wind-up teddy bear that played the drum. Jim hadn't played with the toy for a long time and he eagerly tried out the key, but this time it was too big.

Then, Jim had another idea. "Perhaps the key fits something in the loft," he thought. He was usually too scared to go into the loft on his own because it really was scary. But now he was so determined to find the key's home that he ran up the stairs boldly and opened the door. The loft was dimly lit, dusty and full of cobwebs. The water pipes hissed and creaked and Jim shivered. He began to look under a few dustsheets and opened some old boxes, but didn't find anything that looked like it needed a key to unlock it. Then, he caught sight of a large book sticking out from one of the shelves. It was one of those sorts of books fitted with a lock. Jim lifted down the book, which was extremely heavy, and put it on the floor. His fingers trembled as he put the key in the lock. It fitted perfectly. He turned the key and the lock sprang open, releasing a cloud of dust. Jim wiped the dust from his eyes, slowly opened the book and turned the pages.

What a disappointment! The pages were crammed with tiny writing and there were no pictures at all. Jim was about to shut the book again when he heard a voice. The voice was coming from the book! "You have unlocked my secrets," it said. "Step into my pages if you are looking for adventure."

Jim was so curious that he found himself stepping on to the book. As soon as he put his foot on the pages he found himself falling through the book. The next thing he knew he was on the deck of a ship. He looked up and saw a tattered black flag flying from a flagpole and on the flag were a skull and crossbones. He was on a pirate ship! He looked down and saw that he was dressed like a pirate.

The pirate ship was sailing along nicely, when suddenly Jim saw some dangerous-looking rocks in the water – and they were heading straight for them! Before he could shout, the ship had run aground and all the pirates were jumping overboard and swimming to the shore. Jim swam, too.

The water felt deliciously warm and when he reached the shore he found warm sand between his toes. He couldn't believe it! Here he was on a desert island. The pirates went in all directions, searching for something to make a shelter. Jim looked, too, and under a rock he found a book. The book looked familiar to Jim. He was sure he'd seen it somewhere before. He was still puzzling over it when one of the pirates came running towards him waving a knife. "You thief, you stole me rubies!" cursed the pirate in a menacing voice. What was Jim to do?

Then, he heard a voice call out from the book, "Quick! Step into my pages." Without thinking twice, Jim stepped into the book and suddenly he was back in the loft again.

Jim peered closely at the page from which he'd just stepped.
The Pirates and the Stolen Treasure it said at the top of the page.
Jim read the page and found he was reading exactly the adventure
he had been in. He turned excitedly to the contents page at the
front of the book and read the chapter titles. *Journey to Mars*,
he read, and *The Castle Under the Sea*. Further down it said:
The Magic Car and *Into the Jungle*. Jim was thrilled. He realized
that he could open the book at any page and become part of the
adventure and he only had to find the book and step into it to get
back to the loft again.

After that, Jim had many, many adventures. He made lots of
friends in the stories and he had lots of narrow escapes. But he
always found the book again just in time. Jim was never
lonely again.

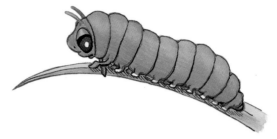

The Jealous Caterpillar

One spring day, a green caterpillar sat on a leaf. He watched a beautiful butterfly flutter past him on the breeze. "It's not fair. Here I am stuck on this boring leaf with nothing to do and nowhere to go while that lucky creature can fly across the world and see far-off lands," thought the caterpillar crossly. "And what's more," he continued to himself, "not only has that butterfly got wings with which to fly, but he's beautiful, too. Look at poor me. I'm just a dull green. No one will notice me because I'm the same colour as the leaf." The caterpillar really did feel very sorry for himself and rather jealous. "Go and enjoy yourself. Don't worry about me," he called spitefully to the butterfly.

But the butterfly hadn't heard a single word the caterpillar had been muttering and soon he flew away. The caterpillar suddenly decided that he was going to be like the butterfly. "I'll learn how to fly and I'll paint myself lovely colours so that I look beautiful, too," he thought. He looked around for something to paint himself with but, of course, there was nothing at all on the leaf. Then, he tried to fly. He launched himself from his leaf and tried to flap his tail, but all he did was land on the leaf below.

Along came a ladybird. "Aha!" thought the caterpillar. "Here's a beautiful creature who knows how to fly. I'll ask her to teach me." So the caterpillar said, "Hello, I've been admiring your beautiful wing case. Could you tell me how I, too, could be beautiful? And can you teach me to fly?"

The ladybird looked at the caterpillar. "Be patient and wait a while," she said wisely, "and soon enough you'll get what you want." And with that the ladybird went on her way.

"Whatever can she mean? She's just too proud to teach me," the caterpillar thought jealously.

Some time later, a bee buzzed past and landed on a nearby leaf. "Aha!" thought the caterpillar. "Here's a beautiful creature who knows how to fly. I'll ask him to teach me." So the caterpillar said, "Hello, I've been admiring your beautiful striped back. Could you tell me how I, too, could be beautiful? And can you teach me to fly?"

The bee looked at the caterpillar. "You'll find out soon enough, young man," said the bee sternly. And with that he went on his way.

"Whatever can he mean? He's just too haughty to teach me," the caterpillar thought jealously.

A while later, along came a bird. "Aha!" thought the caterpillar once more. "Here's a beautiful creature who knows how to fly. I'll ask him to teach me." So once again the caterpillar said, "Hello, I've been admiring your beautiful feathers. Could you tell me how I, too, could be beautiful? And can you teach me to fly?"

The bird looked at the caterpillar and thought to himself slyly that here was a very silly caterpillar, but he would make a tasty snack for his chicks. "Let's see if I can trick him," he thought.

"I can't give you wings and I can't make you beautiful. But I can show you the world. I expect you'd like to see the world, wouldn't you, little caterpillar?" said the bird.

"Oh, yes!" said the caterpillar in great excitement.

"Climb upon my back then, little caterpillar!" said the crafty bird.

The caterpillar did as he was told and the bird flew off towards his nest. At first, the caterpillar clung tightly to the bird's back but soon he felt quite sleepy and eventually he dozed off and slipped from the bird's back. Down he fell through the air and landed on a leaf, but still he didn't wake up. Soon, he was wrapped in a soft, brown, papery cocoon from which he would not wake up for a long while.

Meanwhile, the bird reached his nest. "Look at the treat I've brought you," he said to his chicks.

They looked very puzzled. "What treat, Dad?" one of them piped up.

"This nice juicy caterpillar," said the bird, shaking the feathers on his back. "Climb down, little caterpillar," he said. But of course there was nothing there. Now, it was the father's turn to look puzzled, while the chicks laughed at him.

"Well, I must have dropped him," he said. "I've never done that before," he added. He flew out of the nest in search of the caterpillar but he was nowhere to be seen. Once, he saw a strange brown, papery parcel on a leaf, but in the end the bird had to return to the nest with his beak empty.

A long while later, the caterpillar woke up. "I must get out of this stuffy wrapping," he thought, as he pushed his way out. He stood on the leaf and yawned and stretched. As he stretched, he noticed to his amazement two pairs of beautiful wings spreading out on either side of his body. "Are they really mine?" he wondered. He tried lifting and turning them and yes, he could make them work. He looked at his reflection in a raindrop and saw a lovely butterfly staring back at him. "So the ladybird and the bee were right," he exclaimed. "How foolish I was to be a jealous caterpillar," he declared to a passing ant, "for now I am a beautiful butterfly after all."

Esmerelda the Ragdoll

At the back of the toy cupboard on a dark and dusty shelf lay
Esmerelda the ragdoll. She lay on her back and stared at the
shelf above, as she had done for a very long time. It seemed to
Esmerelda that it was many years since she had been lifted up
by Clara, her owner, and even longer since she had been out
in the playroom with the other toys. Now, her lovely yellow
hair was all tangled and her beautiful blue dress was creased,
torn and faded. Each time Clara opened the toy cupboard door,
Esmerelda hoped very much that she would be chosen, but Clara
always played with the newer toys at the front of the cupboard.
Every time Clara put her toys back in the cupboard, Esmerelda
felt herself being pushed further towards the back. It was very
uncomfortable and indeed, Esmerelda might have suffocated if it
wasn't for a hole at the back of the cupboard, which enabled her
to breathe.

These days Esmerelda felt very lonely. Until recently a one-eyed teddy bear had been beside her on the shelf. Then one day, he had fallen through the hole at the back of the cupboard and was never seen again. Esmerelda missed him dreadfully, for he had been a lovely old teddy with a gentle nature. Now she, too, could feel herself being pushed towards the hole. She felt a mixture of excitement and fright at the prospect of falling through it. Sometimes, she imagined that she would land on a soft feather bed belonging to a little girl who would really love her. At other times she thought that the hole led to a terrifying land full of monsters.

One day, Esmerelda heard Clara's mother say, "Now Clara, today you must tidy up the toy cupboard and clear out all those old toys you no longer play with."

Esmerelda could see Clara's small hands reaching into the cupboard. She couldn't bear the thought of being picked up by the little girl and then discarded. "There's only one thing to do," she said to herself. She wriggled towards the hole, closed her eyes and jumped. Esmerelda felt herself falling and then she landed with a bump on something soft.

"Watch out, my dear!" said a familiar voice from underneath her. Esmerelda opened her eyes and saw that she had landed on One-eyed Ted.

The two toys were so overjoyed to see each other again that they hugged one another. "What shall we do now?" cried Esmerelda.

"I have an idea," said Ted. "There's a rusty old toy car over there. I wanted to escape in it, but I can't drive with only one eye. What do you think? Shall we give it a go?"

"Yes, yes!" exclaimed Esmerelda, climbing into the driver's seat.

By now, One-eyed Ted had found the key and was winding up the car. "Away we go!" he called as they sped off.

"Where are we going?" shouted Esmerelda.

"To the seaside," replied Ted.

"Which way is it?" asked Esmerelda, holding on to her yellow hair streaming behind her in the wind.

"I don't know. We'll have to ask the way," said Ted.

Rounding a bend, they came across a black cat crossing the road. "Excuse me," called Ted, "could you tell us the way to the seaside?"

Now, as you know, cats hate water. "Whatever do they want to go near water for? Why should I help them?" thought the cat. "It's the other side of that mountain," he growled as he ran off.

On sped the rusty car and up the mountainside. When they reached the top of the mountain they met a sheep. Now, as you know, sheep never listen properly. "Excuse me," said Esmerelda, "where can we find the beach?"

Well, the silly sheep thought Esmerelda was asking where they could find a peach! "Down there," she bleated, nodding towards an orchard in the valley below.

Esmerelda and Ted leaped back into the car and sped off down the mountainside, but when they reached the orchard there was no sign of water, of course – just a lot of peach trees.

ESMERELDA THE RAGDOLL

Once again, they scratched their heads in puzzlement. Just then, a mole popped his head out of the Earth. "Excuse me," said Ted, "would you happen to know how we can find the seaside?"

Now, the mole was very wise, but unfortunately he was also, as you know, very short sighted. He peered at Esmerelda's blue dress. "That patch of blue must surely be a river and rivers run into the sea," he thought.

"Just follow that river," he said, "and you'll end up at the seaside. Good day!" And with that he disappeared underground again.

Esmerelda and Ted looked even more puzzled, for there was no sign of a river in the orchard. "Oh well," sighed Esmerelda, "perhaps we'll never find the seaside."

"Don't give up," said Ted. "We'll surely find it in the end." They climbed back in the rusty car and set off again. After a short while the car started to splutter and then it came to a complete halt at the side of the road. "What shall we do now?" cried Esmerelda.

"We'll just have to wait here and see what happens," said Ted. It seemed like a very long time that they sat beside the road. At long last they heard footsteps and then Esmerelda felt herself being picked up.

"Look – it's a dear old tatty ragdoll," said a voice. Esmerelda looked up and saw that she was being carried by a little girl.

Ted and the rusty car had been picked up by the girl's father. "We'll take them home and look after them," the man said.

Now, they were in a real car and before long the toys found themselves in a house. The little girl carried Esmerelda, One-eyed Ted and the rusty car upstairs to her bedroom and put them down on a windowsill. "I'll be back soon," she whispered.

Esmerelda looked out of the window and nearly danced for joy. "Look, look Ted," she shouted. For out of the window she could see the road and beyond the road was a beach and then the sea. "We reached the seaside after all," she cried.

Esmerelda, Ted and the rusty car lived happily in the house beside the sea. Esmerelda's hair was brushed and plaited and she was given a beautiful new dress. Ted had a new eye sewn on and could see properly again. The rusty car was painted and oiled. Most days the little girl took her new toys down to the beach to play with and the days in the dark toy cupboard were soon forgotten. The little girl used to tell her friends the story of how she had found her three best toys lying beside the road one day. And as for the toys, well, they sometimes talked about that strange day when they had such an adventure – and they'd burst out laughing.

Peter Meets a Dragon

Once upon a time, there was a young boy named Peter. He lived in an ordinary house with an ordinary mum and dad, an ordinary sister and an ordinary pet cat, called Jasper. In fact, everything in Peter's life was so ordinary that he sometimes wished that something extraordinary would happen. "Why doesn't a giant come and squash the house flat with his foot?" he wondered, and "If only a pirate would take my sister hostage!" But each day, Peter would wake up in the morning and everything was just the same as it had been the day before.

One morning, Peter woke up to find a very strange smell in the house. Looking out of his bedroom window, he saw that the front lawn was scorched and blackened. There was smoke drifting off the grass and, further away, he could see some bushes ablaze.

Peter rushed downstairs and out of the front door. He ran out of the garden and down the lane following the trail of smoke and burning grass. He grew more and more puzzled, however, as there was no sign of anything that could have caused such a blaze.

Peter was about to run home and tell his mum and dad, when he heard a panting noise coming from the undergrowth. Parting the bushes gently with his hands he found a young creature. It had green, scaly skin, a pair of wings and a long snout full of sharp teeth. Every now and again a little tongue of flame came from its nostrils, setting the grass around it on fire. "A baby dragon!" Peter said to himself, in great surprise. Big tears were rolling out of the dragon's yellow eyes and down its scaly cheeks as it flapped its wings desperately and tried to take off.

When the dragon saw Peter it stopped flapping its wings. "Oh, woe is me!" it sobbed. "Where am I?"

"Where do you want to be?" asked Peter, kneeling down on the scorched ground.

199

"I want to be in Dragonland with my friends," replied the dragon. "We were all flying together, but I just couldn't keep up with them. I got tired and needed a rest. I called to the others but they didn't hear me. Then, I just had to stop and get my breath back. Now I don't know where I am, or if I'll ever see my friends again!" And with that the baby dragon started to cry once more.

"I'm sure I can help. I'll get you home," said Peter, though he had no idea how.

"You?" hissed a voice nearby. "How could you possibly help? You're just a boy!" Peter looked round and to his astonishment found Jasper sitting behind him. "I suppose you're going to wave a magic wand, are you?" continued Jasper. "You need to call in an expert." Then, he turned his back on Peter and the baby dragon and started washing his paws.

Peter was astounded. He'd never heard Jasper talking before. He had thought he was just an ordinary pet cat. "W ... w ... what do you mean?" he stammered.

"Well," said Jasper, glancing over his shoulder at Peter, "I reckon that horse over there could help. Follow me."

So Peter and the baby dragon – whose name was Flame –
followed Jasper over to where the horse stood at the edge of a
field. Jasper leaped up on to the gate and called to the horse. Then,
he whispered in the horse's ear. The horse thought for a moment,
then whispered back in Jasper's ear. "He says he's got a friend on
the other side of the wood who'll help," said Jasper.

"But how?" said Peter, looking perplexed.

"Be patient! Follow me!" said Jasper as he stalked off through
the grass. "And tell your friend to stop setting fire to everything!"
he added. Peter saw, to his horror, that Flame was indeed blazing a
trail through the field.

"I can't help it," cried Flame, about to burst into tears again.
"Every time I get out of breath I start to pant and then I start
breathing fire."

"Let me carry you," said Peter. He picked Flame up in his arms
and ran after Jasper. The baby dragon felt very strange.
His body was all cold and clammy, but his mouth was still
breathing hot smoke, which made Peter's eyes water.

He ran through the wood, just keeping Jasper's upright tail in sight. On the other side of the wood was another field and in the field was a horse. But this was no ordinary horse. Peter stopped dead in his tracks and stared. The horse was pure milky white and from its head grew a single, long horn. "A unicorn!" breathed Peter.

Jasper was already talking to the unicorn. He beckoned with his paw to Peter. "He'll take your friend home and you can go, too, Peter, but don't be late for tea, or you know what your mother will say." And with that, Jasper was off.

"Climb aboard," said the unicorn gently.

Peter and the little dragon scrambled up on to the unicorn's back. "What an adventure," thought Peter. Up, up and away they soared through the clouds.

Flame held tightly on to Peter's hand with his clammy paw. At last, Peter could see a mountain ahead through the clouds. Now they were descending through the clouds again and soon the unicorn landed right at the top of the mountain. "I'm home!" squeaked Flame joyously as they landed. Sure enough, several dragons were running over to greet him. They looked quite friendly, but some of them were rather large and one was breathing a great deal of fire.

"Time for me to go," said Peter a little nervously, as Flame jumped off the unicorn's back and flew to the ground. The unicorn took off again and soon they were back in the field once more.

As he slid off the unicorn's back, Peter turned to thank him, but when he looked he saw that it was just an ordinary horse with no trace of a horn at all. Peter walked back home across the field, but there was no sign of burnt grass. He reached his own front lawn, which was also in perfect condition. Peter felt more and more perplexed. "I hope Jasper can explain," he thought, as the cat ran past him and into the house. "Jasper, I took the baby dragon home. What's happened to the burnt grass?" he blurted out. But Jasper said not a word. He ignored Peter and curled up in his basket.

When Peter wasn't looking, however, Jasper gave him a glance that seemed to say, "Well, was that a big enough adventure for you?"

Cinderella

Once upon a time, there was a beautiful young girl who lived with her widowed father. He had brought her up to be kind and gentle. All went well until the day the girl's father married again. His second wife was very proud of her house. Everything always had to be spotlessly clean. Worse than that, she had two spiteful daughters. All three had terrible tempers and they hated the beautiful young girl with a vengeance. All day long from dawn to dusk she was made to scrub and clean, mend clothes and serve at the table. At night, while the household slept, there was coal to fetch, fires to be laid and the table to be set for breakfast the following day.

The stepmother gave her own two daughters the finest rooms in the house. To her stepdaughter, she gave the coldest loft room, with the hardest bed and a duvet cover that was so thin it barely kept out the winter chill. To keep warm, the poor girl had to sit in the chimney nook of the kitchen with her feet near the cinders. Because of this, her stepsisters nicknamed her Cinderella.

One day, a footman called at the house to deliver an invitation. Cinderella carried it into the dining room where her stepsisters were having breakfast. "What have you there?" shrieked one of them, snatching the envelope from her hand. She tore it open with her long, polished nails. "Ooh!" she cried. "It's an invitation from the Prince to attend a ball tomorrow night!"

The other sister jumped up and down with delight. "We're going to a ball!" she yelled.

"Am I invited, too?" asked Cinderella shyly.

"You?" cried the elder sister.

"You – invited to the palace ball?" cried the other sister and they both burst into fits of laughter. The elder sister, who was very plump, laughed so much that she became quite breathless and had to ask Cinderella to loosen her corset.

205

The sisters spent the next day preparing for the ball. Cinderella was kept very busy, pressing and starching the girls' ballgowns, curling their hair and fixing bows and ribbons. They told her to lace their corsets extra tight to make them look slimmer. She was made to run hither and thither all day. "Fetch my pearl necklace!" called one.

"Polish my party shoes!" demanded the other. At last, both sisters were ready to go and set off by carriage to the ball. "Don't wait up!" they shouted out of the window to Cinderella, as the coach sped away.

Cinderella went back into the kitchen. Now, the house seemed calm and quiet at last. She picked up a broom and danced slowly round the room, imagining that she was at the ball. "How wonderful it would be to go to the ball," she sighed wistfully and sat down by the fire where it was warm and started to cry.

"Don't cry, my child," said a gentle voice.

Cinderella looked up to see a beautiful stranger standing before her. "Who are you?" said Cinderella.

"I am your Fairy Godmother," came the reply. "Now, dry your tears. Would you like to go to the ball?" said the fairy.

"Oh, yes please," cried Cinderella, leaping up.

"Then you shall go," said the fairy. "But first, run into the garden and fetch me a nice fat pumpkin." Cinderella did as she was told. When she returned, the Fairy Godmother tapped the pumpkin with her magic wand and instantly it was transformed into a sparkling glass coach.

"Now we need some horses," said the fairy. At that moment, there was a scuttling noise in the corner of the kitchen and four white mice popped out of a hole. In an instant the Fairy Godmother tapped them with her wand and they became four handsome white horses. "Now what about a footman," she said. Before Cinderella could speak she tapped Cinderella's black cat and there before her very eyes stood a footman. "Now there's just one more thing we need before you go," said the fairy, "and that's a coachman."

Cinderella looked about the kitchen and scratched her head.

  207

Then, she ran into the garden and came back with a live frog. "Will he do?" she asked her Fairy Godmother.

"Indeed he will," replied the fairy, tapping the frog. And suddenly, there was a coachman standing by the coach. "All aboard!" he cried.

Cinderella was just about to leap inside when her Godmother called her back. "I nearly forgot something," she said.

The tip of her wand touched Cinderella's ragged clothes and Cinderella looked down to see, to her astonishment, that she was wearing the most beautiful ballgown that there ever was. At her neck glittered a diamond necklace and on her feet were a dainty pair of glass slippers. "Have a lovely time at the ball," said her Godmother. "But do not stay a minute longer than midnight, for on the stroke of twelve, everything will be as it was before."

And with that, she vanished.

When Cinderella arrived at the ball, she found herself in a dazzling ballroom filled with people. Everyone stopped to stare at this beautiful girl and soon the Prince himself approached and asked her to dance. "Who is she?" people were asking. The Prince and Cinderella danced together all evening. Her stepsisters watched, never once guessing who she was.

"Isn't she beautiful," remarked the elder sister jealously.

"Such a tiny waist – she might snap in two!" whispered the other spitefully and they both roared with laughter.

When the banquet was served the Prince insisted that Cinderella sit next to him and after dinner they danced again. Cinderella was enjoying herself so much she forgot all about the time. It was only when the clock struck midnight that she remembered her Godmother's warning. She fled from the ballroom without a backward glance. The Prince hurried after her but she ran faster than he. As she sped down the steps her ballgown turned to rags and she dropped one of her glass slippers. The Prince picked it up. By the time she reached home, Cinderella was exhausted.

Soon, her sisters arrived home. "There was the most beautiful princess at the ball," said one.

"The Prince fell in love with her and he was deeply saddened when she left at midnight," said the other.

As for the Prince, he spent all night with the glass slipper pressed to his cheek, mourning the loss of the most wonderful girl he had ever set eyes upon. The next morning, he was determined to find her. He sent his servant to all corners of the kingdom. "I will marry the girl whose foot fits the slipper," he declared. Well, every princess, duchess and lady in the land tried on the slipper, but none of them could fit the tiny shoe on her foot.

At last, the servant called at the house of Cinderella and her stepsisters. "Me first!" they cried, pushing each other out of the way. One sister tried on the slipper but her toes were so fat that she couldn't squeeze them into the dainty shoe. Then, the other sister tried, but her toes were so long they wouldn't fit either.

Cinderella had been watching from her corner by the fire. Now, she came forward. "May I try on the shoe?" she asked timidly.

The stepsisters shrieked, "Don't be absurd! You weren't even at the ball."

But the prince's servant said, "If you wish to try on the slipper, then you shall." Cinderella slid her foot into the glass slipper and of course it fitted perfectly. The stepsisters were completely speechless with rage.

At that moment, there was a flash of bright light and Cinderella's Fairy Godmother appeared. She touched Cinderella with her magic wand and immediately the girl's rags were transformed into the ballgown that she had worn the night before. Then, her sisters recognized the beautiful Princess they had seen at the ball. They fell upon their knees and begged forgiveness for the way they had treated her, hoping that they, too, might be invited to the palace. The servant escorted Cinderella to the palace and when the Prince saw her, he immediately asked her to marry him. At the wedding there was much rejoicing and the sisters were so well behaved that they, too, received marriage proposals and they all lived happily ever after.

Mr Squirrel Won't Sleep

It was autumn. The leaves were falling from the trees in the forest and there was a cold nip in the air. All the animals began to get ready for winter.

One night, Mr Fox came back from hunting and said to his wife, "There's not much food about now it's getting colder. We'd better start storing what we can to help tide us over the winter."

"You're right, Mr Fox," replied his wife, as she gathered her cubs into their lair.

"I'd love to go fishing," said Mr Bear, "but I'll have to wait until spring now." He went into his den, shut the door tight and sealed it.

"Well, I'm off for a holiday in the Sun," announced Mrs Cuckoo, preening her feathers. "See you all next year!" she called, as she took to the wing and flew south.

Mrs Mouse ran by with a mouthful of straw. "Must dash," she squeaked, "or my winter bed will never be finished in time." But soon she, too, was curled up with her tail wrapped around her for warmth.

Now, only Mr Squirrel wasn't ready for winter. He danced about in his tree, leaping from branch to branch and chasing his tail. "Ha, ha!" he boasted. "I don't have to get ready for winter. I have a fine store of nuts hidden away, a beautiful bushy tail to keep me warm and besides, I don't feel in the least bit sleepy." And he carried on playing in his tree.

"Are you still awake?" snapped Mr Fox.

"Go to sleep!" growled Mr Bear.

"Please be quiet," squeaked Mrs Mouse, drawing her tail more tightly about her ears.

But Mr Squirrel wouldn't go to sleep. Not a bit of it. He danced up and down all the more and shouted, "I'm having SUCH FUN!" at the top of his voice.

Winter came. The wind whistled in the trees' bare branches, the sky turned grey and it became bitterly cold. Then, it started to snow. At first, Mr Squirrel had a grand time making snowballs – but there was no one around to throw them at and he began to feel rather lonely. Soon, he felt cold and hungry, too.

"No problem!" he said to himself. "I'll have some nice nuts to eat. Now, where did I bury them?" He scampered down his tree to find that the ground was deep with snow. He ran this way and that trying to find his hiding places, but all the forest looked the same in the snow and soon he was hopelessly lost.

"Whatever shall I do?" he whimpered, for now he was shivering with cold and hunger and his beautiful, bushy tail was all wet and bedraggled.

All of a sudden he thought he heard a small voice. But where was it coming from? He looked all around but there was no sign of anyone. Then, he realized that the voice was coming from under the snow. "Hurry up!" said the voice. "You can join me down here, but you'll have to dig a path to my door."

Mr Squirrel started digging frantically with his front paws and sure enough there was a path leading to a door under a tree stump. The door was slightly open – open enough for Mr Squirrel to squeeze his thin, tired body through.

Inside was a warm, cosy room with a roaring fire and sitting by the fire was a tiny elf. "I heard you running around up there and thought you might be in need of a bit of shelter," said the elf. "Come and warm yourself by the fire." Mr Squirrel was only too pleased to accept and soon he was feeling warm and dry.

"This isn't my house, you know," said the elf. "I think it might be part of an old badgers' sett. I got lost in the forest and so when I found this place, I decided to stay here until spring. Though how I'll ever find my way home, I don't know." A fat tear rolled down the elf's cheek.

"I have been a very foolish squirrel," said Mr Squirrel. "If you hadn't taken me in I surely would have died. I am indebted to you and if you will let me stay here until spring, I will help you find your way home."

"Of course you can stay," replied the elf. "I'd be glad of the company." So Mr Squirrel settled down with his tail for a blanket and soon he was fast asleep.

Days and nights passed, until one day, the elf popped his head out of the door and exclaimed, "The snow has melted, spring is coming. Wake up, Mr Squirrel." Mr Squirrel rubbed his eyes and looked out. It was true. There were patches of blue in the sky and he could hear a bird singing.

"Climb upon my back," Mr Squirrel said to the elf. "I'm going to show you the world." They set off through the forest until they came to the highest tree of all.

"Hold tight!" called Mr Squirrel, as he climbed up through the branches until finally they reached the very top of the tree.

"You can look now," said Mr Squirrel, seeing that the elf had put his tiny hands over his eyes. The elf uncovered his eyes and stared and stared. He had never seen anything like it in his whole life. Stretching in all directions, as far as the eye could see, were mountains, lakes, rivers, forests and fields.

"What's that silvery-blue thing in the distance?" asked the elf.

"Why, that's the sea!" replied Mr Squirrel.

Suddenly, the elf started to jump for joy.

"What is it?" said Mr Squirrel.

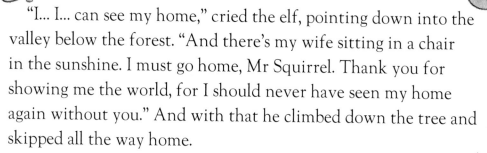

"I... I... can see my home," cried the elf, pointing down into the valley below the forest. "And there's my wife sitting in a chair in the sunshine. I must go home, Mr Squirrel. Thank you for showing me the world, for I should never have seen my home again without you." And with that he climbed down the tree and skipped all the way home.

Mr Squirrel made his way back to his own tree.

"Where have you been?" said Mr Fox.

"We've been looking for you," said Mr Bear.

"I'm glad you're home," said Mrs Mouse.

"So am I," said Mr Squirrel. "I've been very foolish, but I've learned my lesson. Now let's have a party – I've got rather a lot of nuts that need eating up!"

So the animals celebrated spring with a fine feast. And Mr Squirrel vowed not to be silly again next winter.

The Missing Scarf

Kanga was very proud of her stripy knitted scarf. She had made it herself and she had also made a smaller matching one for her son, Joey. Kanga used to hop through the bush with her scarf streaming out behind her, while Joey's could just be seen poking out of the top of her pouch. Now, Joey was older, he was too big for Kanga's pouch, but he still wore his scarf as he hopped along beside his mother.

Then one day, Kanga woke up to find that her beautiful scarf was missing. She searched high and low but it was nowhere to be found. Eventually, she decided that she would have to go out into the bush to look for it.

"Stay here," she said to Joey. "I'll try not to be long. I'm sure to find my scarf soon." Kanga hopped off into the bush and started to search among the roots of trees and under stones.

She had gone quite a long way when, looking up into the branches of a eucalyptus tree, she spotted Koala. Now, Koala was usually to be found asleep, but this time she was busy preparing a meal of eucalyptus leaves for her children. Kanga looked up at Koala and then her jaw dropped. For Koala was quite clearly wearing Kanga's scarf around her tummy. Then, to Kanga's horror, she saw Koala use the end of the scarf to wipe the teacups! "Koala," Kanga called. "Whatever do you think you're doing?"

Koala stopped cleaning the teacups and looked down through the branches of the eucalyptus tree at Kanga. "I'm wiping my teacups with my apron," she replied sleepily, "and I'll thank you not to interfere!" And with that, she yawned and moved several branches further up the tree.

219

Poor Kanga felt very embarrassed. How could she have mistaken Koala's striped apron for her own scarf? She hopped away and carried on further into the bush. After a while she could hear Kookaburra's familiar laughing call nearby. "I know," thought Kanga, "I'll ask her if she's seen my scarf. She'd be able to spot it easily from up in the sky." She followed the sound of Kookaburra's call until she came to the tree where she lived. She looked up and, sure enough, there was Kookaburra flying towards the tree. Kanga was about to call up when her jaw dropped again. For Kookaburra was quite clearly carrying Kanga's scarf in her beak. "Kookaburra," Kanga called. "Whatever do you think you're doing?"

"I'm lining my nest," mumbled Kookaburra through a beakful of stripy feathers. "And I'll thank you not to interfere," she added more distinctly, for she had now reached the nest and was arranging the feathers carefully in place.

220

Poor Kanga felt even more embarrassed. How could she have mistaken the feathers for her own scarf? She hopped away and carried on further into the bush. After a while she reached a wide open plain and there she saw Emu running past with his baby chicks on his back. As he rushed past, Kanga's jaw dropped yet again. For Emu quite clearly had Kanga's scarf tucked in among his chicks. "Emu," called Kanga. "Whatever do you think you're doing?"

"I'm taking my chicks to safety," said Emu, glancing up at the sky as he sped away. "And you'd be wise to do the same," he added. Then, Kanga realized that what she had thought was her rolled-up scarf were just the striped chicks on Emu's back.

Poor Kanga felt even more embarrassed. How could she have made such a mistake? Then, she felt a few spots of rain on her nose and, looking up, saw a huge black cloud overhead. There was no time to lose – she must find shelter.

221

She made a dash for some trees at the edge of the plain and soon found herself by a stream. She wandered along beside the stream feeling cold, wet, tired and miserable. Finally, she lay down in the wet grass beside the stream and tried to get to sleep. She shivered with cold and wondered how Joey was and whether he was behaving himself. She so hoped he hadn't got into mischief.

Just then, there was a tap on her shoulder and there stood Platypus. "I could hear you in my burrow over there," she said pointing towards a hole beside the stream just above the water. "I thought you might like this to keep you warm," she added.

"My scarf!" exclaimed Kanga.

"Oh, is that what it is? I'm ever so sorry," said Platypus. "I've been using it as a blanket for my babies. It's rather cold and damp in my burrow, you know," she added, rather forlornly. "Where did you find it?" asked Kanga.

"It was stuck on some thorns and I know I shouldn't have taken it, but I just thought it would be so nice for keeping my young ones warm," blurted Platypus and she started to sob.

222

"There now," said Kanga, "don't cry. You can keep the scarf. You need it more than me."

Platypus stopped crying and looked overjoyed. "Thank you," she said.

"No, thank you," said Kanga. "I've learned a lesson, which is not to get upset over a scarf, for I've ended up falling out with my friends."

Kanga made her way back home, but it took a long time because she apologized to all her friends on the way. When she explained what had happened Emu, Kookaburra and Koala all forgave her and by the time she reached home she was feeling much better. Joey was there to greet her. "What have you been up to while I was away?" she asked.

"I made you this," he said. He handed her a scarf. It was a very funny-looking scarf, made out of twigs, grass and feathers, but Kanga loved it very much.

"This is much more special than my old scarf," she said. And she gave Joey an extra big hug.

The Bear and the
Ice Kingdom

Once upon a time, a king ruled a far-off land. It was a sunny, pleasant kingdom with lush forests, green meadows and sparkling rivers. The King of this land had a daughter he loved very much and who one day would rule the kingdom.

Beyond the King's land was another kingdom, but this one was very different. It was an icy-cold place with wind-swept, snowy plains and cold, frozen seas. The Sun never warmed this kingdom and it was always winter. Anyone or anything venturing into the kingdom was immediately turned to ice by the cold. This kingdom was ruled by a wicked ogre, whose wish was to own the warm lands of his neighbour.

One day, the wicked ogre thought of a cunning plan to capture the kingdom he desired. He decided he would kidnap the king's daughter. Once she had entered the wicked ogre's ice kingdom she, too, would be turned to ice. In time, the King would die and, as there would be no one to inherit his kingdom, the wicked ogre could seize it.

So one day, the wicked ogre left his own cold kingdom and travelled to the other kingdom disguised as a merchant. He carried a big bag containing some samples of cloth and some jewellery. The wicked ogre came to the castle gates and asked if he might show the Princess his wares. She agreed and showed him to a room where he laid out the cloth and jewellery on a table. But as soon as she started to look at the wares, the wicked ogre bundled her up in the bag and carried her off.

As soon as the Princess felt the cold chill of the wicked ogre's kingdom, she was immediately frozen to ice.

The wicked ogre thought that all he now had to do was wait for the King to die of old age or a broken heart and the kingdom would be his. But despite the cunning of the wicked ogre, his evil deed had been spotted by one of the king's courtiers. The King immediately sent his troops to the ice kingdom to rescue his daughter. But as soon as they reached the kingdom they, too, were frozen to ice.

The King was in despair. There seemed to be no way to get his beloved daughter back. Then one day, he thought of an idea. He sent out a royal proclamation to every part of his land. It said that anyone who could rescue his daughter would be granted any gift within the King's power to bestow.

Many adventurers tried to rescue the king's daughter, in the hope that they might win her hand in marriage, or be granted riches and lands as a reward. But each who ventured into the evil ogre's ice kingdom met the same fate. All were turned to ice.

Then one day, the king's dancing bear read the royal proclamation and asked to speak with the King. "Your Majesty," said the dancing bear, "I have a plan to rescue your daughter, the Princess."

"And what is your plan?" asked the King.

"My plan is a secret, Your Majesty," said the dancing bear. "But if you will trust me, I promise she will be brought safely home."

The King agreed to let the dancing bear try and rescue his daughter. After all, every other attempt had ended in failure so what did he have to lose? The dancing bear was released from his chain and went off immediately to begin his task. He travelled day and night until finally he reached his destination – a cold, snowy place where his cousin lived. His cousin was not like the dancing bear, however. The dancing bear was small and brown, but his cousin was big and white. This bear loved the cold and snow, for he had a thick fur coat. He was a Polar bear.

The dancing bear told his cousin what had befallen the king's daughter. The Polar bear agreed to rescue her. The dancing bear couldn't wait to get going, for his cousin's snowy home was much too cold for him. Eventually, they arrived back in the King's land and the Polar bear set off alone to try and rescue the Princess.

Soon, he reached the wicked ogre's ice kingdom. A freezing, icy wind blew all around the Polar bear, but his thick, warm fur coat kept out the cold. Then, a huge snow storm came up, but the Polar bear just shook his fur and all the snow fell from him. On went the Polar bear until he reached the wicked ogre's castle.

The ogre never expected that anyone would be able to enter his cold kingdom without being turned to ice, so he never even locked his doors. While the ogre was snoring in his bedroom, the Polar bear searched stealthily around the castle until he found the frozen Princess. He gently gathered her up and they were just about to make their escape when the ogre awoke.

As the wicked ogre tried to snatch the Princess away from the Polar bear, the Polar bear dealt the wicked ogre a mighty blow with his paw. The wicked ogre fell down dead. The Polar bear then carried the Princess away from the icy kingdom. As soon as she entered her father's warm kingdom again, she returned to life.

There was much rejoicing at the return of the king's daughter, of course, and the first thing the King did was to summon the dancing bear to him.

"You have kept you promise," the King said, "and now I will keep mine. What is your wish?"

"All I ask, Your Majesty, is that I am freed to roam the forests of your kingdom."

The King immediately granted his wish. And as a reward to the Polar bear, he was given the ice kingdom as his own domain which, being so cold, suited him just fine!

The Toys That Ran Away

"Put your toys away, Lucy," said Lucy's mother from the kitchen, "it's time to get ready for bed."

Lucy gave a great big sigh. "Do I really have to?" she asked, knowing full well what the answer was going to be.

"Yes, of course you do," said her mother. "You shouldn't have to be told each time to put your toys away. You really don't look after them properly."

It was true. Lucy never had been very good at looking after her toys. Once, she left her beautiful new doll outside in her pram and she had become ruined after it rained. Then, she had carelessly dropped her tea set on the floor and some of the cups had broken. And she was forever just pushing all her toys back

in the cupboard in a hurry, instead of putting them away carefully. Worse still, when she was in a temper, she would throw her toys and sometimes she would even kick them.

Tonight, Lucy was in another of her 'can't be bothered' moods. She grabbed a handful of toys and threw them into the cupboard. In first went some dolls, which all landed on their heads and then fell in a heap. Next, Lucy threw in the little tables and chairs from the doll's house. They landed with a bounce and came to a stop in the corner. Without even looking behind her, Lucy then picked up some puzzles and a skipping rope and tossed them into the cupboard, too. They landed with a crash on the floor of the cupboard as well.

"That's that," said Lucy. She closed the cupboard door, squashing the toys even more, and went into the bathroom to have her bath.

Inside the toy cupboard, Teddy, one of the toys, spoke. "I'm not going to stay here a moment longer," he said.

"Nor me," said Katie the ragdoll.

231

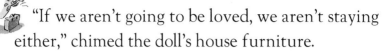
"If we aren't going to be loved, we aren't staying either," chimed the doll's house furniture.

"I want to be somewhere where I'm not thrown around," said one of the puzzles.

"So do we," said the roller blades.

One after another, all the toys agreed that they weren't going to stay. They decided they would all go back to Toyland and wait to be given to some children who would love them more.

The next morning, Lucy decided that she would play with her skipping rope. When she opened the toy cupboard, she couldn't believe her eyes. All the toys had vanished. The shelves were completely empty.

At first, Lucy thought her mother had moved them, but her mother said she hadn't. "I expect you've put them somewhere yourself, Lucy, and can't remember where you've left them," said her mother, not very helpfully. All day, Lucy searched high and low for her missing toys, but they were nowhere to be found. She went to bed in tears that night, wondering if she would ever be able to play with her toys again. She was already missing them terribly.

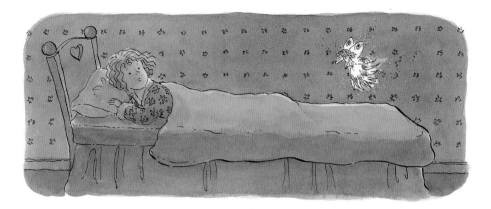

That night, Lucy was suddenly woken by a noise in her bedroom. Was she seeing things or was that a little fairy at the bottom of her bed? "Who are you?" asked Lucy.

"I am the special messenger from Toyland," replied the fairy. "I have been sent to tell you that all your toys have run away back to Toyland, because you treated them badly."

"Oh, I do miss my toys so much," cried Lucy.

"Well, if you really do, then you had better come and tell them yourself," said the fairy.

With that, the fairy floated over to Lucy and took her hand. The fairy then beat her wings so fast that they became a blur. At the same time Lucy felt herself being lifted from her bed. Out of Lucy's bedroom window they both flew, across fields and forests, until it became too misty for Lucy to see anything at all.

Suddenly, they were floating down to the ground. The mist lifted and Lucy found herself in the grounds of a huge fairy-tale castle with tall, pointed turrets and warm, yellow lights twinkling from the windows.

233

"This is Toyland Castle," exclaimed the fairy, as she led Lucy to a large red door.

The fairy knocked on the door. "Do enter, please," said a voice.

Lucy found herself in a large, cosy room with a huge log fire. Sitting in the corner was a kindly looking little man wearing a carpenter's apron and holding a broken wooden doll. "Hello," he said, "you've come to ask your toys to return, haven't you?"

"Well ... er ... yes," said Lucy, not really quite knowing what to say.

"It's up to them to decide, of course," said the little man. "They only come back here if they are mistreated. If they are broken, I repair them and then they go to other children who love them more."

"But I *do* love my toys," wept Lucy.

"Then come and tell them yourself," smiled the little man.

He led Lucy into another room and there, to her surprise, were all her toys. Not only that, but they were all shiny and new again. Nothing was broken or chipped or scratched.

Lucy ran up to her toys. "Please, toys, please come home again.

I really do love you and miss you and I promise I shall never mistreat you again," she cried. She picked up Teddy and gave him a big hug. Then, she did the same thing to all the other toys.

"Well, it's up to the toys now," said the little man. "You must go back home again with the fairy messenger and hope that they will give you another chance."

With that, the fairy messenger took Lucy's hand and soon they were floating over her own garden again and through her bedroom window. Lucy was so tired she didn't even remember falling asleep when she got into bed.

In the morning she awoke, still rather sleepy, and rushed to the toy cupboard. There, neatly lined up on the shelves, were all her toys. Lucy was overjoyed. From that day on, she always treated her toys well and took great care of them.

Lucy never was quite sure whether the whole thing was a dream or not, but it certainly did the trick whatever it was. There was one thing that really puzzled her though. If it had just been a dream, why were all the toys so shiny and new again?

The Castle in the Clouds

There was once a family that lived in a little house in a village at the bottom of a mountain. At the top of the mountain was a great, grey castle made of granite. The castle was always shrouded in clouds, so it was known as the castle in the clouds. From the village you could only just see the outline of its high walls and turrets. No one in the village ever went near the castle, for it looked such a gloomy and forbidding place.

Now, in this family there were seven children. One by one, they went out into the world to seek their fortune and at last it was the youngest child's turn. His name was Sam. His only possession was a pet cat named Jess and she was an excellent rat-catcher. Sam was most upset at the thought of leaving Jess behind when he went off to find work, but then he had an idea.

"I'll offer Jess' services at the castle in the clouds. They're bound to need a good ratter and I'm sure I can find work there, too," he thought.

His parents were dismayed to discover that Sam intended to seek work at the castle, but try as they might they could not change his mind. So Sam set off for the castle with Jess at his side. Soon, the road started to wind up the mountainside through thick pine forests. It grew cold and misty. Rounding a bend they suddenly found themselves up against a massive, grey stone wall. They followed the curve of the wall until they came to the castle door.

Sam went up to the door and banged on it. The sound echoed spookily. "Who goes there?" said a voice.

Looking up, Sam saw that a window high in the wall had been thrown open and a face was eyeing him suspiciously.

237

"I... I... I wondered if you'd be interested in employing my cat as a rat-catcher," began Sam.

The window slammed shut, but a moment later, a hand beckoned him through the partly open castle door. Stepping inside, Sam and Jess found themselves face-to-face with an old man. "Rat-catcher, did you say?" said the old man raising one eyebrow. "Very well, but she'd better do a good job or my master will punish us all!"

Sam sent Jess off to prove her worth. In the meantime, Sam asked the old man, who was the castle guard, if there might be any work for him, too.

"You can help out in the kitchens. It's hard work, mind!" the guard said.

Sam was soon at work in the kitchens – and what hard work it was! He spent all day peeling vegetables, cleaning pans and scrubbing the floor. By midnight he was exhausted. He was about to find a patch of straw to make his bed, when he noticed Jess wasn't around. He set off in search of her. Down dark passages he went, up winding staircases, looking in every corner and behind every door, but there was no sign of her. By now, he was hopelessly lost and was wondering how he would ever find his way back to the kitchens, when he caught sight of Jess' green eyes shining like lanterns at the top of a rickety spiral staircase. "Here, Jess!" called Sam softly. But Jess stayed just where she was.

When he reached her, he found that she was sitting outside a door and seemed to be listening to something on the other side. Sam put his ear to the door. He could hear the sound of sobbing. He knocked gently at the door. "Who is it?" said a girl's voice.

"I'm Sam, the kitchen boy. What's the matter? Can I come in?" said Sam.

"If only you could," sobbed the voice. "I'm Princess Rose. When my father died my uncle locked me in here so that he could steal the castle. Now I fear I shall never escape!"

Sam pushed and pushed at the door, but to no avail. "Don't worry," he said, "I'll get you out of here."

Sam knew exactly what to do, for when he had been talking to the guard, he had spotted a set of keys hanging on a nail in the rafters high above the old man's head. He had wondered at the time why anyone should put keys out of the reach of any human hand. Now, he thought he knew – but first he had to get the keys himself!

Sam and Jess finally made their way back to where the keys were, only to find the guard was fast asleep in his chair right underneath them! Quick as a flash, Jess had leaped up on to the shelf behind his head. From there, she climbed higher and higher until she reached the rafters.

She took the keys in her jaws and carried them gingerly down. But as she jumped from the shelf again, she knocked over a jug and sent it crashing to the floor. The guard woke with a start. "Who goes there?" he growled. He just caught sight of the tip of Jess' tail as she made a dash for the door.

Sam and Jess retraced their steps with the guard in hot pursuit. "You go a different way," hissed Sam, running up the stairs to Rose's door, while the old man disappeared off after Jess. Sam put one of the keys in the lock. It fitted! He turned the key and opened the door. There stood the loveliest girl he had ever seen. The Princess ran towards him, as he cried, "Quick!

240

There's not a moment to lose." He grabbed her hand and led her out of the tower.

"Give me the keys," she said. She led him down to the castle cellars. At last, they came to a tiny door. The Princess put the second key in the lock and the door opened. Inside was a small cupboard and inside that was a golden box filled with precious jewels. "My own box – stolen by my uncle," cried Rose.

Grabbing the box the pair ran to the stables and saddled a horse. Suddenly, Jess appeared with the guard still chasing him. With a mighty leap Jess landed on the back of the horse behind the Princess and Sam. "Off we go!" cried Sam.

And that was the last that any of them saw of the castle in the clouds. Sam married the Princess and they all lived happily ever after.

Jack and the Beanstalk

Once, there was an old woman who lived with her only son, Jack in a tumble-down cottage in a meadow by a pine forest. The old woman and her son were very poor and they were getting poorer as each winter passed. After one particularly cruel and cold winter, when the ground had frozen like ice, the old woman turned to her son and said, "Jack, there is only one thing left to sell. You must take the old brown cow to market tomorrow and sell her – she is all that is left between us and starvation, so mind you get a good price!"

So the next morning, Jack took the old brown cow and started the long journey into town.

Halfway through his journey, Jack stopped to eat his crust of bread. Just then, a farmer passed by and stopped to chat. After Jack told the farmer where he was heading and why, the farmer looked at the old cow and scratched his chin thoughtfully. He put his hand into his pocket and said to Jack, "I'll swap you these dried beans for your old brown cow."

Jack looked at the beans in the farmer's hand and shook his head. "I'm sorry," he said, "but I must take the old brown cow to sell at the market so that my mother and I can buy bread."

The farmer promised Jack that if he would swap the cow for the beans, Jack would make his fortune. Jack finally agreed and went home with the beans in his pocket.

When he got home he told his mother about his adventure, but his mother cried when Jack told her the old brown cow was gone and all they had were dried beans. She snatched the beans from Jack's hand and threw them out of the window in anger.

243

Just as dawn was breaking, Jack woke up to discover a huge beanstalk had shot up during the night right outside his window. He ran downstairs and looked at the huge beanstalk – it was taller than even the tallest trees in the nearby pine forest and disappeared into the clouds. Jack decided to climb the beanstalk.

Jack climbed and climbed. He climbed so high that when he looked down, the tumble-down cottage was a tiny speck far below. The top of the beanstalk was still out of sight so he climbed some more. Eventually, Jack climbed through the clouds and was amazed when he got to the top of the stalk to discover another land very different from the one he'd left below.

Everything was HUGE. The trees were enormous, the grass came up to Jack's shoulder and in the distance was the largest castle he had ever seen. Just as Jack was starting out towards the castle, he heard a thunderous rustling in the grass behind him and he looked round to see a huge giantess towering above him.

"Mmmmm – not much meat on those bones," she said, "so I won't bother to eat you. However, you might come in handy around the house to do all the boring old chores." And with that she picked Jack up, popped him into the pocket of her apron and carried him into the castle. On the way, she warned Jack not to let her husband, the giant, see him. "The last house boy I had was made into jam and he's looking for another to pound into bread," she said quite calmly.

Soon, Jack felt the castle shudder at the approach of the giant and he hid behind the coal scuttle. "Fee Fi Fo Fum," roared the giant. "I smell the blood of an Englishman. Be him live or be him dead, I'll break his bones to make my bread."

"Don't be silly," said the giantess, "you've never once changed your socks and it's your feet you can smell."

Satisfied with this answer, the giant sat down and started to count his money. Jack sneaked a peek from his hiding place and saw a mountain of gold coins piled high on the table. Then, the giant scooped it all back into the purse, put his feet on the table and fell sound asleep.

When the thunderous snores convinced Jack that it was safe, he sneaked up on to the table. The purse was within reach and Jack dragged it to the edge of the table where it fell with a tremendous KLUNK on to the floor. The giant slept on. Quickly Jack climbed down and dragged the purse to the castle door and down to the meadow and then down, down, down the beanstalk.

When Jack finally got back with his treasure he showed it to his mother who hugged him with joy and warned him never to climb the beanstalk again.

But Jack decided that he would go back to the castle to find some more treasures and when morning came again he got dressed and went down to the beanstalk to start the long climb all over again. Before he left the house, he tied a red scarf around his head and painted freckles on his face, so that when he reached the top of the beanstalk and once again met the giantess, she would not recognize him.

246

Once again, she picked Jack up,
popped him into her apron pocket and
warned him about the terrible giant.
Once more, Jack hid as the castle trembled
at the giant's approach.

"Fee Fi Fo Fum," roared the giant, "I smell the blood
of an Englishman. Be him live or be him dead, I'll break his bones
to make my bread."

"Tsk tsk," said the giantess, "the only thing you can smell is
your armpits which have never been washed."

Satisfied with this answer, the giant sat down and called for
his hen to be brought to him. Jack peeked around and saw to his
amazement that the hen had laid a beautiful golden egg! Before
long, the giant rested his head once more, then fell fast asleep.

When Jack heard the snoring, he sneaked up on to the table
and gently took the hen, then quickly climbed down and carried
it to the castle door and down to the meadow and then down,
down, down the beanstalk. When Jack returned once more with
his treasure, his mother was waiting for him and when Jack
showed her the hen, she hugged him and begged him
never to climb the beanstalk again.

But once again, Jack thought about the
treasures in the castle and the following
morning he went down to the beanstalk to
start the long climb all over again.

This time before he left the house, he tied a blue scarf around his head and rubbed dirt into his face and once again when he reached the top of the beanstalk and met the giantess, she did not recognize him. As before, she picked Jack up, popped him into her apron pocket and warned him about the giant.

Again, the castle trembled at the approach of the giant. "Fee Fi Fo Fum. I smell the blood of an Englishman. Be him live or be him dead, I'll break his bones to make my bread," said the giant once again.

"What rot!" said the giantess. "That'll be all those bugs in your hair that's never been combed!"

Once more satisfied, the giant sat down and called for his harp to be brought to him. When the giant plucked at the strings of the harp, it magically started to sing in a clear soprano voice! The giant was soon lulled into a deep slumber across the table and Jack wanted the beautiful harp so much that he didn't even wait for the snores! Jack climbed up to the table and put his hands on the harp to sneak it from under the nose of the sleeping giant, but to his horror, the harp started to shriek, "Help! Help! I'm being stolen."

The giant woke up. With a mighty roar he shouted, "Fee Fi Fo Fum, I smell the blood of an Englishman. Be him live or be him dead, I'll break his bones to make my bread." And with that he raced after Jack. But the giant wasn't as nimble as Jack and Jack was able to rush out of the castle, down to the meadow and reach the top of the beanstalk with the giant in pursuit.

Jack climbed down as quickly as possible, but the giant was not far behind him. The further down Jack climbed, the closer the giant got to him. When Jack was nearly at the bottom, he called to his mother to fetch the wood axe and then Jack jumped the rest of the way to the ground. He grabbed at the axe and started to chop furiously at the stalk. The giant was almost down when the beanstalk crashed to the ground – right on top of him! The giant was squashed to nothing.

Now, with all the gold they had, Jack and his mother never needed to worry about money again.

Rusty's Big Day

Long ago, there lived a poor farmer called Fred, who had a horse called Rusty. Once, Rusty had been a good, strong horse. He had willingly pulled the plough and taken his master into town to sell his vegetables. Now, he was too old to work on the farm, but the farmer couldn't bear to think of getting rid of him because he was so sweet-natured. "It would be like turning away one of my own family," Fred used to say. Rusty spent his days grazing in the corner of the field. He was quite content, but he felt sad that he was no longer able to help the poor farmer earn his living.

One day, Fred decided to go to town to sell a few vegetables. He harnessed Beauty, the young mare, to the wagon and off they went. Beauty shook her fine mane and tossed a glance at Rusty, as if to say, "Look who's Queen of the farmyard!"

While Fred was in the town, his eye was caught by a notice pinned to a tree. It said:

Horse Parade at 2 pm today
The winner will pull the King's carriage
to the Grand Banquet tonight

"There's not a moment to lose, my girl!" said Fred. "We must get you ready for the parade." So saying, he turned the wagon around. "Giddy-up, Beauty!" he called and she trotted all the way back to the farm.

Fred set to work to make Beauty look more lovely than she had ever done before. He scrubbed her hoofs and brushed her coat until it shone. Then, he plaited her mane and tied it with a bright red ribbon. Rusty watched from the field. "How fine she looks," he thought, wistfully. "She's sure to win." He felt a bit sad that he was too old to take part in the parade, so he found a patch of the sweetest grass to graze on, to console himself.

251

All at once, he heard Fred approach. "Come on, old boy," he said, "you can come, too. It'll be fun for you to watch the parade, won't it?" Rusty was thrilled. It seemed such a long time since the master had last taken him into town. Fred brushed Rusty's coat, too. "You want to look your best, don't you now, old boy?" he said.

Soon, the three of them set off back into town, with Fred riding on Beauty's back and Rusty walking by their side. When they reached the parade ground, there were already a lot of horses gathered there with their owners. There were horses of every shape and size – small, skinny ones, big, muscular ones and there were even big, skinny ones, too!

Soon, it was time for the parade to begin. The King entered the parade ground, followed by the members of the royal court. They took their places at one end of the ground. Then, the King announced three contests. First, there would be a race. The horses would gallop from one end of the parade ground

252

to the other. Then, there would be a contest of strength. Each horse would have to try and pull a heavy carriage. Lastly, there would be a trotting competition. Each horse would have to carry a rider around the parade ground.

The competition began. All the horses lined up at the starting line. "Come on, Rusty. Have a go!" whispered Fred. He led Rusty and Beauty to where the other horses were lined up.

All the other horses turned and stared. "What's an old horse like you doing taking part in a contest like this?" one of them asked disdainfully.

"You won't make it past the starting line!" taunted another.

Rusty said nothing and took his place at the start. Then, they were off down the field. Rusty felt his heart pounding and his feet fly like never before, but try as he might he just couldn't keep up with the others and came in last.

"What did you expect?" snorted the other horses turning their backs on poor old Rusty.

However, Rusty was not downcast. "Speed isn't everything," he said to himself.

253

Now, it was time for the test of strength. One by one, the horses took it in turns to pull the carriage. When it was Rusty's turn, he tried his best. He felt every muscle in his aching body strain, as he slowly pulled the carriage along.

"Not a hope!" declared the other horses.

"Strength isn't everything," said Rusty to himself.

Next, it was time for the trotting competition. "I shall ride each horse in turn," declared the King. He climbed up on to the first horse, but it bolted away so fast that the King was left hanging by the stirrups. The next horse lifted his legs so high that he threw the King right up in the air and he might have hurt himself badly, if he hadn't been caught by one of his courtiers. The next horse was so nervous about carrying the King that his teeth chattered and the King had to put his fingers in his ears. Then, it was Beauty's turn and she carried the King magnificently, until she stumbled at the end. At last, it was Rusty's turn. The other horses sniggered, "Let's see that old horse make a fool of himself!"

Rusty carried the King quite slowly and steadily, making sure he picked his feet up carefully, so that His Royal Highness would not be jolted. "Thank you for a most pleasant ride," said the King dismounting. There was a hush as the horses and their owners awaited the result of the contest. "I have decided," announced the King, "that Rusty is the winner. Not only did he give me a most comfortable ride, but he accepted his other defeats with dignity. Speed and strength are not everything, you know."

Rusty and Fred were overjoyed and even Beauty offered her congratulations. "Though I might have won if I hadn't stumbled," she muttered.

So Rusty proudly pulled the King's carriage that evening and he made such a good job of it that the King asked him if he would do it again the following year. Then, the King asked Fred if his daughter could ride Beauty from time to time. He even gave Fred a bag of gold to pay for the horses' upkeep. So the three of them were happy as they never had been before as they returned home to the farm that night.

The Wrong Kind of Puppy

There was only one thing in the whole world that Peter wanted and that was a puppy. Not just any puppy, but a puppy like the ones he had seen at the local dog show. They were lovely brown, fluffy puppies with big, bright, brown eyes and wagging tails. Peter had spent all day at the show stroking the puppies and they had spent all their time on their back legs wanting to be stroked even more!

Best of all, Peter's parents had promised him a puppy of his very own for his birthday. He could hardly wait. "Please can we get one like those lovely brown ones we saw at the dog show?" he pleaded.

Peter's father shook his head and replied, "I'm sorry, son, but those were very expensive puppies and they grow into very big dogs. We just couldn't afford one of those. But we will get you a puppy, I promise, and I'm sure you'll love it just as much."

Well, Peter was heartbroken. He had no idea that the puppies he had seen were expensive, but he just couldn't imagine loving any other sort of dog.

Eventually, Peter's birthday came around. In the morning, he woke up early to find a big pile of presents from his aunts, uncles and little sister. But where was his puppy? He was just about to burst into tears when he saw that one of the presents was from his parents. It was a big square box, but it certainly didn't feel like there was a puppy inside. He opened the box anyway and discovered that it contained a collar, a lead, a dog bowl, a brush and comb and some bone-shaped biscuits. But still there was no puppy! Without opening any of his other presents, her ran into his parent's room (who were still asleep!) and asked where his puppy was.

"We have to go and collect it today," said his mother. "We've chosen you a lovely little puppy from the dogs' home that desperately needed a new family to look after it. We can go and get it as soon as we've had breakfast."

Peter was much too excited to eat any breakfast, of course, and spent the next half an hour saying, "Can we go yet?" Eventually, everyone was ready and they all climbed into the car for the journey to the dogs' home. Peter sat in the back clutching the lead and hoping it wouldn't be too long before there was a puppy attached to the other end of it!

Soon, they reached the dogs' home and one of the kennel maids took them to where Peter's puppy was being kept. But when Peter first set eyes on the puppy, his heart sank. This wasn't anything like the sort of puppy he had wanted. Instead of being brown and fluffy and bouncy, this puppy was tiny and scraggy and timid. When it saw Peter and his family approach, it gave a little wag of its tail but then just stood in its cage whimpering.

Now, Peter had been taught by his parents that you must never be ungrateful for presents, even if they aren't exactly what you wanted. So although he was very disappointed, he reached out and stroked the puppy. The little scruffy puppy timidly approached Peter, licked his hand and then ran off into the corner of the cage.

"He'll soon get used to you," said the kennel maid brightly. "Come on, Rags, time to go to your new home." And with that, she lifted the little puppy up and placed him in Peter's arms.

All the way home, the little puppy sat quietly in Peter's arms, occasionally trembling. Now and again, he looked up at Peter with his big, soft eyes.

When they got Rags home, he was so frightened that he ran and hid under the curtains. Peter wondered how he was going to be able to play with such a timid friend.

259

Later that day, Peter was sitting at the table having lunch when he felt something cold and wet against his leg; it was Rags' nose. He peered down to see Rags looking up at him, his tail wagging backwards and forwards. "He's looking a bit happier now," said Peter's father. "It will only be a matter of time before he feels really at home here."

The next morning, Peter hurried downstairs as soon as he awoke to say good morning to Rags – because the truth was, although Rags wasn't quite like the puppy he had expected, he was really getting very fond of him.

Rags jumped out of his basket when he saw Peter, his tail

wagging furiously. "He's quite a waggy dog after all," thought Peter. Then, Rags picked up his ball and began to play with it. Every time Peter tried to take it, Rags scurried off with a wag of his tail, looking round to make sure that Peter was chasing him. He seemed to like playing after all!

As the days went by, Rags seemed to grow more and more playful. He would jump up and greet his family with a big lick and a wagging tail, he always wanted to go for walks and to play and he was very quick to learn tricks.

Peter just couldn't believe how much Rags had changed from the timid little creature in the dogs' home to the happy, playful puppy he was now – all thanks to a little love and care.

But the most curious thing of all was the puppy's appearance. He had now grown a beautiful, fluffy coat and, if Peter wasn't very much mistaken, it was quite brown, too. And it matched the colour of his big, brown eyes.

Morag the Witch

Morag was just an ordinary witch – until the day she enrolled for a course of advanced spell casting at the Wizard, Witch and Warlock Institute of Magic. For that was where she met Professor Fizzlestick. Now, Professor Fizzlestick was a very wise old man indeed. Morag, on the other hand, was a very vain young witch who didn't know as much as she thought she did. She could turn people into frogs if they really deserved it, and do other simple spells like that, but she still had a lot to learn. The problem was, Morag thought she was the most perfect little witch in the whole wide world.

Morag's adventure started on her very first day at school. At the beginning of the day, after all the young witches and wizards had made friends and met the teachers, they were called in one by one to talk to Professor Fizzlestick.

"Now, young Morag Bendlebaum, I taught both your mother and your father," said the professor in a very serious voice, "and a very fine witch and wizard they turned out to be, too. So, what kind of witch do you think you are going to be?"

Without giving this any thought at all, Morag blurted out, "I'm better than my parents and I'm probably better than you!"

This answer surprised even Morag, for although she thought this was true, she didn't actually mean to say it.

"Don't be surprised by your answers," said Professor Fizzlestick, "there is a truth spell in this room and whatever you truly believe you must say. And I have to say that you appear to have an enormously high opinion of yourself. Why don't you tell me what makes you so very good?"

"I'm clever," said Morag, "and I'm good, and I'm always right."

"But what about your dark side?" said Professor Fizzlestick.

"I'm sorry to disappoint you," replied Morag quite seriously, "but I'm afraid I simply don't have a dark side."

263

"Well in that case I would like you to meet someone very close to you," said Professor Fizzlestick with a smile on his lips.

Morag looked over to where Professor Fizzlestick pointed and was startled to see on the sofa next to her ... herself!

As Morag stared open-mouthed with astonishment, the professor explained that if, as she believed, she was without a dark side, then there was absolutely nothing to worry about.

"If, however," he continued, "you have deceived yourself, then I'm afraid you are in for a few surprises."

With that, the professor dismissed them both from the room and told them to get to know each other. As Morag and her dark side stood outside the professor's room, Morag's dark side jumped and whooped for joy. "At last," she cried, "I'm free. I don't have to sit and listen to you telling me what's right all day; I don't have to keep persuading you to choose the biggest slice of cake before your brother – in fact, I don't, I repeat **don't,** have to do anything that you tell me at all."

So saying, she broke into a run and rushed down the corridor, knocking over chairs and bumping into other little witches and wizards along the way. Morag was horrified. She would have to follow her dark side and stop her from causing trouble. Morag chased after her dark side and finally caught up with her at the chocolate machine. "Don't eat all that chocolate," cried Morag. "You know it's bad for your teeth and will ruin your appetite for lunch!"

"Tsk!" scoffed her dark side. "You might not want any chocolate but I certainly do!" And with that she ran off once more, dropping chocolate on to the freshly polished floor, as well as pushing a big piece into her mouth.

Just then, the bell sounded for lunch. Although Morag felt she ought to find her dark side, she also knew that the bell was a command to go to the dining hall and she mustn't disobey it. Morag sat down to lunch next to her friend, Topaz. She was just about to tell her what had happened, when she saw that Topaz was not eating her vegetables! Morag scolded Topaz for this and gave her a lecture on eating healthily.

Topaz stared at Morag in amazement, then peered closely at her. "What's happened to you?" she asked.

Morag explained what had happened in Professor Fizzlestick's office and then declared, "And you know, it's the best thing that has ever happened to me. I thought I was good before, but now I'm even better. I never want my dark side back again, but we must find her and lock her up so that she can do no harm."

Topaz agreed that they must find her dark side, but secretly hoped that she and Morag would be re-united. Morag wasn't Morag without her dark side.

After lunch, Morag went for her first lesson of the afternoon. When she walked into the classroom she discovered her dark side already there, busy preparing spells! Morag's dark side had already prepared a 'turning a nose into an elephant's trunk' spell and a 'turning skin into dragons' scales' spell and was just finishing off a 'turning your teacher into stone' spell!

Morag suddenly heard a trumpeting noise from the back of the classroom. She turned to find that the wizard twins, Denzil and Dorian Dillydally, had both sprouted huge grey trunks down to the ground where their noses had been. Morag rushed over to her dark side to make her change them back, but before she could reach her she tripped over a creature crouching down on the floor. It looked just like a dragon and it was wearing a purple and white spotted dress last seen on Betina Bumblebag. Morag's dark side was casting spells all over the place. "Oh, why doesn't the teacher stop her!" cried Morag to Topaz.

I'm sure you've guessed by now. Nice Miss Chuckle was entirely turned to stone from head to foot!

Just then, Professor Fizzlestick walked into the classroom. Morag pointed to her dark side, still making spells at the front of the classroom.

266

Lock her up immediately," Morag begged the professor.

"I'm afraid that you are the only one who can do that," said the wise old man. "The two of you are inseparable and you need each other. Without your dark side you would be unbearable and without you she is dreadful. Have I your permission to lock her back inside you?"

Even though Morag didn't want any part of her dark side back, she agreed reluctantly. Her dark side instantly disappeared and Morag felt … wonderful! Oh, it was so good to be back to normal, to be basically good, but occasionally mischievous.

"Thank you," said Morag to the professor. "I think I've learned something very valuable today."

"There is good and bad in everyone," replied the professor, "even the most perfect of witches."

Morag blushed when she remembered what she had said earlier that morning, but she was so relieved to find she was normal that she really didn't mind. Morag and Topaz went back to the classroom to undo all the bad things Morag's dark side had done, but on the way they both felt a huge urge for a snack, so they stopped at the chocolate machine first!

The Dog With No Voice

There once lived a prince whose words were pure poetry. He amused the court with his witty, rhyming verse, yet his kind and thoughtful words made him popular with all. It was said he could even charm the birds from the trees.

One day, he was walking in the forest when he came upon an old lady with a huge bundle on her back. "Let me help," said the Prince. He took the load and walked along beside the woman. They chatted away and before long they had reached the old lady's door.

Now, the old lady – who was really a witch – had been listening intently to the Prince's words. "What a fine voice he has!" she thought to herself. "I would like my own son to speak like that. Then maybe he could find himself a wealthy wife and we'd be rich for ever more!"

"You must be thirsty," she said to the Prince. "Let me give you something to quench your thirst to repay you for your kindness." The Prince gratefully accepted and was given a delicious drink which he drained to the last drop. He was about to thank the witch when he began to feel very peculiar. He found he was getting smaller and smaller. He looked down at his feet and saw two hairy paws. Then, he turned round and saw to his horror that he had grown a shaggy tail! He tried to shout at the witch but all that came out of his mouth was a loud bark!

The witch hugged herself for joy. "My spell worked!" she cackled. "Come here my son!" she called.

There appeared at the door a rough-looking young man. "What's going on, my dearest mother?" he said in a voice that sounded familiar to the Prince. Then, he looked down and exclaimed, "Where did you find this poor little dog?"

Now, the Prince understood what had happened. "The old lady has turned me into a humble hound and given my voice to her son. Whatever am I to do?" he thought miserably. "I can't return to the palace. They'll never let a stray dog in." He turned with his tail between his legs and trotted off forlornly into the forest.

The witch and her son were delighted with his new voice. She made him scrub himself clean from top to toe and dressed him in the Prince's clothes. "Now go," she said, "and don't return until you've found a rich girl to marry!"

The young man set off, eager to try out his new voice. Soon, he was feeling very pleased with himself as he talked to passers-by. "What a very polite young man!" and "What a wonderful way with words," people cried. "He could charm the birds out of the trees," other people said.

The witch's son travelled far and wide until at last he came to a castle where he spied a fair Princess sitting on her balcony. He called to her and straight away she arose and looked down into the garden, enraptured by the sound of his beautiful voice. She

was enchanted by his fine words and guessed they must belong
to a prince. Soon, the Princess and the witch's son were chatting
away merrily and to his delight when he asked her to marry
him she readily agreed. "For one with so beautiful a voice," she
thought to herself, "must indeed be a fine young man."

Meanwhile, the poor Dog-Prince wandered in the forest,
surviving as best he could by foraging for roots and fruits in the
undergrowth. Feeling truly miserable, he stopped to drink from
a stream. As he dipped his long dog's tongue in the cool water, he
caught sight of someone sitting on a bridge. It was a pixie, fishing
with a tiny net.

"Cheer up!" said the little fellow, "I saw everything that happened and I think I know how we can get your voice back. Follow me!" And with that he was off, dancing away through the forest with the Dog-Prince trotting along behind. They seemed to go on forever and the Dog-Prince was feeling very hot, and the pads of his paws were quite sore, by the time they reached the castle. He could see the witch's son in the garden calling to the Princess on the balcony. The Dog-Prince's eyes filled with tears, for she was quite the loveliest girl he had ever seen and he wished he could marry her himself.

"We will be married today," the witch's son was saying in the Prince's voice, "I will await you by the church, my fairest one." Seizing his fishing net, the pixie leaped high in the air. As the words 'my fairest one' floated up to the balcony, he caught them in the net and gave them back to the Dog-Prince.

As soon as he had swallowed the words, the Dog-Prince could speak again. "Thank you, little pixie," he cried, "but what can I do? Now I am a dog with a prince's voice. The Princess will never marry me."

"If you want to break the witch's spell, you must go to the church – fast!" said the pixie. And with those words he disappeared.

Straight away, the Dog-Prince ran to the church door. There was the Princess looking most perplexed, for standing beside her was the witch's son – with not a word in his head. "I don't understand," she cried, "I thought I was to marry a silver-tongued young man, but now I find he is a dumb ragamuffin!"

"I can explain," exclaimed the Dog-Prince.

The Princess spun around. "Who can explain?" she asked, for all she could see was a dog in front of her. "What a handsome dog!" she cried, bending down and kissing him on the nose. To her astonishment, the dog's hairy paws and shaggy tail immediately disappeared and there stood the Prince. "But you're ... but he ..." she stammered looking from the Prince to the witch's son.

Well, the Prince explained everything that had happened and after that he and the Princess were married with great rejoicing. And as for the witch's son? He wasn't a bad young man, really, so the Prince taught him to speak again – with a beautiful voice – and he married the princess' younger sister.

273

The Three Little Pigs

Once upon a time, there were three little pigs who lived on a farm with their mother and father. They decided that, although they were just little pigs, they were quite grown up enough to make their way in the big wide world, so one day they set off together to make their fortunes.

After they had walked for quite some time, one of the little pigs started to feel rather tired. Just then, a farmer went by on his haycart.

"Please may I buy some straw to build a house?" asked the little pig. "This hay is light enough and soft enough for my house." And with that his brothers left the little pig with his pile of hay and carried on their journey.

A little further down the road, the second little pig grew very tired. Just then, they passed by a forester cutting wood.

"Would you sell me some of your wood?" asked the second little pig. "This wood isn't too heavy and it isn't too rough for my house – it's just right." And with that the third little pig carried on his journey. Soon, even the third little pig grew very tired and up ahead he spotted a builder making a wall out of stone.

"Aha," he thought, "that's exactly what I need to build my house, as it's strong and tough, just like me." And so he bought some stone and built himself a house.

That evening, just as the first little pig was settling comfortably in his bed of hay, he heard a rustling outside the house. He easily parted the hay with his hands to look outside and gulped in fright when he saw the big bad wolf looking at him greedily.

"Little piggy, little piggy, will you let me in?"

"Not on the hairs of my chinny chin chin, I will not let you in," shuddered the first little pig.

"Then I'll huff, and I'll puff, and I'll blow your house down," said the big bad wolf.

And sure enough, he gave a little huff, and he gave a little puff, and with very little effort he blew the house down. Before the straw had settled to the ground, the little pig ran away as fast as his little legs would carry him to the home of his nearest brother.

The next evening, just as the two brothers were sitting down at their wooden table to eat their dinner, they heard scratching and sniffing outside the house. They peeked through the wooden window and gasped in alarm when they saw the big bad wolf staring at them hungrily. His stomach rumbled loudly.

"Little piggies, little piggies, will you let me in?"

"Not on the hairs of our chinny chin chins, we will not let you in," trembled the little pigs.

"Then I'll huff, and I'll puff, and I'll blow your house down," said the big bad wolf.

And sure enough, he huffed a bit, and he puffed a bit, and with a bit of effort he blew the house down. Before the planks of wood had crashed to the ground, the two pigs ran away as fast as their little legs would carry them to the home of their brother.

The next evening, just as the three brothers were making the fire to warm their toes, they heard crunching and crashing outside the house. The third little pig pulled a tiny stone out of the wall to make a peephole and they all shrieked in terror when they saw the big bad wolf staring at them ravenously. His stomach grumbled even louder and he was smacking his lips with glee at the feast waiting just a short breath away!

"Little piggies, little piggies, will you let me in?"

"Not on the hairs of our chinny chin chins, we will not let you in," quaked the three little pigs.

"Then I'll huff, and I'll puff, and I'll blow your house down," said the big bad wolf.

And sure enough, he took a big huff, and he took a big puff, and with a big effort he blew. But the house didn't blow down. So he took a bigger huff, and he took a bigger puff, and with the biggest of efforts he blew. But the house still didn't blow down. So he filled his lungs as full as he could and with a mighty effort he blew and blew and blew! And the house stayed up!

With that the big bad wolf started to climb up the stone wall to the chimney on the roof. The three little pigs looked around the stark stone room and then at each other in dismay – there was nowhere in here to hide and nowhere left to run. They would have to stand and fight the big bad wolf!

Suddenly, one of the little pigs had an idea and whispered it into the ears of his brothers. They all ran over to the fireplace and hooked a huge pot of water over the roaring fire. They heard the wolf climb into the chimney. The water in the pot started to steam. They heard the wolf climbing down the chimney. The water started to bubble. They heard the wolf slide the rest of the way down the chimney and he landed splash in the middle of the pot of now boiling water. PLOP!

"AAARRRRHHHHH!" screamed the big bad wolf, leaping immediately out of the boiling pot. The three little pigs ran around the room trying to get away from the wolf, as the big bad wolf ran around the room trying to cool down, until eventually he ran straight through the stone wall, leaving a huge big bad wolf shaped hole, and carried on running and screaming and shouting all the way through the woods. That was the last they ever saw of the big bad wolf.

The three little pigs knew they had beaten the wolf and he would never trouble them again, so they decided to build a brand new, comfortable house to live in. They built the walls of tough, strong stone. They made tables of smooth, warm wood and they gathered lots of sweet-smelling, soft fresh hay to make comfortable beds. It was the best house in the world and they all lived in it happily ever after.

Bobby's Best Birthday Present

It was the morning of Bobby's birthday and he was very excited.
When he came down to breakfast, there on the table was a big
pile of presents. Bobby opened them one by one. There was a
beautiful book with pictures of wild animals, a toy racing car and
a cap. Bobby was very pleased with his presents, but where was
the present from his parents? "Close your eyes and hold out your
hands!" said his mother. When he opened his eyes there was a
large rectangular parcel in his hands. Bobby tore off the wrapping
and inside was a box. And inside the box was a wonderful, shiny,
electric train set.

For a moment, Bobby looked at the train set lying in the box. It was so lovely he could hardly bear to touch it. There was an engine and six carriages all lying neatly on their sides. Bobby carefully lifted the engine out of the box. Then, he set up the track and soon he had the train whizzing round his bedroom floor. Freddie the cat came in and watched the train going round. Round and round he watched it go, then one time when the train came past him he swiped at it with his paw and derailed it. The engine and the six carriages came tumbling off the track and landed in a heap on the floor. "Look what you've done!" wailed Bobby, as he picked up the train and reassembled it. The carriages were undamaged, but the engine had hit the side of his bed and was badly dented.

Bobby was very upset. "My brand new train is ruined!" he cried.

"Don't worry, Bobby," said his mother, "we can't take it back to the shop now, but we can take it to the toymender in the morning. I'm sure he'll make a good job of mending the engine and it'll look as good as new again." Bobby played with his racing car, he wore his new cap and he read his new book, but really all he wanted to do was to play with his train set. He went to bed that night with the engine on the floor near his bed.

In the morning, when Bobby woke up, the first thing he did was to look at the poor broken engine of his train set. He picked it up, expecting to see the buckled metal, but the engine was perfect. He couldn't believe his eyes! He ran to his parents. "Look, look!" he cried. They were as amazed as he was. The engine worked perfectly and Bobby played happily with his train set all day – but he made sure Freddie kept out of his room!

That night, Bobby couldn't sleep. He lay in bed tossing and turning. Then, he heard a noise. It was the sound of his train set rushing round the track. He peered into the darkness and yes, he could definitely make out the shape of the train as it sped by. How had the train started? It couldn't start all by itself! Had Freddie crept into his room and flicked the switch? As his eyes gradually became accustomed to the dark, Bobby could make out several shapes in the carriages. Who were the mysterious passengers? He slid out of bed and on to the floor beside the train set. Now, he could see that the passengers were little people wearing strange pointed hats and leafy costumes. "Elves!" thought Bobby.

At that moment, one of the elves spotted Bobby. "Hello there!" he called as the train rushed past again. "We saw that your train set was broken. We so much wanted a ride that we fixed it. I hope you don't mind!" Bobby was too astounded to say anything at all. "Come with us for a ride," called the elf as his carriage approached again.

As the train passed him the elf leaned out of the carriage and grabbed Bobby by the hand. Bobby felt himself shrinking as he flew through the air and the next instant he was sitting beside the elf in the carriage of his very own train set! "Here we go – hold tight!" called the elf, as the train left the track and went out through the window into the night sky.

"Now, where would you like to go? What would you like to see?" asked the elf.

"Toyland!" replied Bobby without hesitation. Sure enough, the train headed towards a track which curved up a mountain made of pink and white sugar. Beside the track were toys going about their daily business. Bobby saw a ragdoll getting into a shiny tin car. Then, a wooden sailor puppet wound up the car with a large key and off went the doll. He saw three teddy bears setting off for school with their satchels on their backs. Then, he saw a brightly coloured clown playing a drum.

The train stopped and Bobby and the elves got out. "Now for some fun!" said one of the elves. They had come to a halt by a toy fairground. Bobby found that this was like no other fairground he had ever been to before. For in Toyland, all the rides are real. The horses on the carousel were real horses. The dodgem cars were real cars. And when he got in the rocket for the rocket ride, it took him all the way to the Moon and back!

"Time to go, Bobby," said one of the elves at last. "It'll be morning soon." Bobby climbed wearily back into the train and soon he was fast asleep. When he woke up it was morning and he was back in his bed. The train set lay quite still on its tracks. But in one of the carriages was a scrap of paper and on the paper, in tiny spidery writing, were the words: *We hope you enjoyed your trip to Toyland – the elves.*

Maurice the Minnow's Dangerous Journey

Maurice the minnow lived in a beautiful, reed-fringed pond in a clearing in the middle of a small woodland. He had been born one fine spring morning and now he spent each day swimming happily in the shallows with all his little minnow brothers and sisters.

But life in the pond had its dangers, too! He had heard alarming stories about a kingfisher that would dive into the water from a branch overhanging the pond and grab tiny fish and swallow them down. And then there was the heron – a great, grey, stalking bird that suddenly loomed into the shallows and snatched unsuspecting fish with its great beak.

But the stories Maurice feared most were the ones about Lucius the pike. Lucius had lived in the pond for longer than anyone could remember. Woe betide you if you met Lucius when he was hungry, for he would dart out from his hiding place among the water weeds, and you would be gone! Nothing ever escaped from his huge jaws, which were lined with needle-sharp teeth. Maurice had heard tales of Lucius swallowing fish bigger than Maurice could imagine – not to mention ducks, voles and other animals of the pond. Why, there was even a rumour that Lucius had once snatched a dog from the bank and taken it down to the depths of the pond to devour it!

Maurice's mother had said that the best way to avoid meeting Lucius was to always stay in the shallows and never swim across the pond, for it was in the deep, dark waters that Lucius loved to hunt.

289

One sunny summer's day, Maurice and his brothers and sisters were swimming in the shallows as usual, when suddenly he felt himself being lifted up and out of the water. The next thing he knew he was flapping helplessly in the bottom of a net, gasping for breath. Mercifully, he soon found himself back in the water again, but it seemed different now. It was light all around and there were no welcoming, sheltering weeds to hide in. And where were all his brothers and sisters? Next, to his horror, he saw a huge, unfamiliar creature staring at him. He'd heard no stories about anything as big as this! The creature's head seemed so close that Maurice felt certain he was about to be eaten. But just as suddenly, the creature seemed to move away and Maurice felt himself being carried along in this new, strange, watery world.

Maurice was wondering if he was to be trapped in this new, small pond forever when just as suddenly as he seemed to have entered the pond, he was now leaving it again. He felt himself

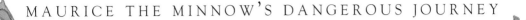

falling down, down, until – with a splash – he was back in his own pond again. Or at least, it seemed like his pond, but nothing was quite as familiar as it had been. Finding a clump of water weed, he immediately dived under it for safety, while he considered what to do next.

"Hello, you're new here, aren't you?" a friendly voice said. Maurice looked round in surprise to find himself face to face with a frog. He told the frog about his horrible adventure while the frog listened patiently, nodding wisely from time to time.

"Well, we know what's happened to you, don't we?" said the frog when Maurice had finished. "You got caught in a little boy's fishing net. They're often about around here. I've no doubt the big creature you saw was just the little boy looking at you swimming in his jam jar full of water. And now he's decided to put you back. The only trouble is, you're far from home. You live on the other side of the pond. And to get you back means we have got to go on a very dangerous journey."

Maurice didn't like the sound of this at all, but he missed his family terribly and knew that he would never be able to get back home without the kind frog's help. So without more ado, the two of them set off for their journey across the deep, dark pond.

"Swim near the surface. It's safer," advised the frog, "but keep a close eye out for kingfishers."

They seemed to have been swimming for ages, when suddenly a great, dark shadow appeared beneath them.

"It's Lucius!" cried the frog in fright.

Before either of them could escape, they found themselves face to face with the dreaded pike. "Well, well," leered Lucius. "I can't believe my luck! A frog *and* a minnow. Lunch and supper together if I'm not mistaken!"

So saying, he opened his enormous jaws and was about to swallow them whole when – BOINK! – a huge, flat stone landed right on Lucius' head. Dazed, Lucius sank slowly towards the bottom of the pond.

"Quick! It's our chance to escape!" yelled the frog. The two friends swam for their lives. Maurice kept thinking that any moment Lucius would reappear, but he needn't have worried. Lucius had too big a headache to think about hunting for a while yet!

Then suddenly, Maurice was home. He recognized his own little part of the pond and there swimming in the shallows was his family.

"I can't thank you enough," said Maurice gratefully to the frog. "But what *did* happen to Lucius?"

"You can thank the little boy who caught you in the net for our escape," said the frog. "He was skimming stones across the pond and luckily Lucius' head got in the way!"

Maurice decided that he'd had quite enough adventures for one day and found himself a cosy piece of water weed to hide under. Soon, he was fast asleep.

The Mirror of Dreams

The house on the corner of Nightingale Avenue was tall and very handsome and was by far the largest in the neighbourhood. From the street you could see four floors of beautifully decorated rooms and if you peeped over the railings you could see the basement below. If you were lucky enough to be asked into the house, and passed through the beautiful hallways into the playroom, you might meet the owner's daughter, Cordelia. Sometimes, Cordelia would be sitting in her silk pyjamas playing on her grand piano and sometimes she would be dressed in the finest velvet gowns playing with her lovely dolls.

If you went down the stairs and into the basement, you might come across Polly. Polly's mother was a maid in the house, and worked hard all day long to make the house sparkling clean. Sometimes, Polly helped her to polish the ornaments and dust the furniture, but more often Polly sat on her own in her small bedroom drawing pictures with some crayons on a drawing pad she had been given for her birthday. When Polly was helping to polish the furniture she would look longingly at all of Cordelia's

294

fine clothes and toys and when she sat alone in her room she would draw pictures of all the beautiful things she would like to own if only she could afford them.

One day, a large parcel was delivered to the house and taken upstairs to Cordelia's bedroom. A little while later, Cordelia's maid carried a pretty, ornate mirror down from her room and put it with the rubbish waiting for collection outside the house. Polly asked the maid why the mirror was to be thrown away and the maid explained that Cordelia had been given a new mirror in which to brush her long, silky locks and that she didn't need it any more. The maid then asked if Polly would like the old mirror and of course Polly accepted with pleasure – it was the most beautiful thing she had ever owned.

Polly carried the mirror back to her room and polished it lovingly. As she polished the glass a strange thing started to happen. The glass went misty and then cleared as her own reflection stared back at her once more. But the reflection that stared back was not dressed in rags and worn old clothes as Polly was, but in a rich gown of the most beautiful cream satin, with pink bows and apricot lace.

Polly was entranced. She looked almost as beautiful as Cordelia! Her hair gleamed and her fingers were white and magnificent. As she looked further into the mirror, she saw herself dancing at a ball and then sitting down to eat the finest food she had ever seen – hams and roasted meats, and cakes of strawberries and cream!

And then the mirror spoke to her. "I am the Mirror of Dreams," the cool, clear voice said. "Whatever your heart desires most will be reflected in my shiny surface."

Polly was astounded, but so happy. She didn't care that it was only a daydream, for when she saw her reflection in the beautiful clothes, she felt as if she were truly there dancing and eating the fine foods – she could almost taste the fruit and cream in her mouth!

From that day on, Polly sat in her room every day and dreamed and dreamed and dreamed. She had never felt so happy before and could not wait to wake up each morning to visit her

imaginary world. She certainly didn't understand how Cordelia could have thrown away such a magical wonder and thought that she could not have known of its enchanting secret. She supposed also that Cordelia could have had no use for such a mirror, for whatever Cordelia wanted in real life she received, and would have no need to dream. But Polly was to find out that this was very far from true!

Weeks passed and every day Polly sat and dreamed of ermine cloaks, of diamonds and pearls, of parties and picnics and carnivals. Eventually, she had dreamed every dream she had ever wanted. And Polly began to realize that it no longer made her as happy as it once had and she began to grow weary of her Mirror of Dreams. She sat in front of the mirror less and less and eventually when she did visit the mirror she could not think of a single thing that would make her happy. Even the dreams she had in which her mother wore fine silk clothes and didn't have to scrub and clean for their living could no longer make her happy.

She preferred her real mother, who came to kiss her good night and read her stories no matter how tired and overworked she was. Eventually, she stopped looking in the mirror altogether and finally decided to throw the mirror away – it had only made her more unhappy.

As the long winter turned into spring she acted upon her decision and took down the mirror to throw away with the rubbish. But as she looked into the glass, it misted over in its familiar way and she saw herself in the mirror as she looked in real life, but in it she was playing with other children like herself and reading stories with them and sharing toys. She felt gloriously happy and knew in that instant that all she wanted was a very good friend. She realized in that moment, too, that perhaps Cordelia really had known the mirror's secret, but that she also had become more unhappy as the dreams faded and reality forced itself upon her. She wondered aloud what it was that Cordelia had dreamed of and for the second and last time the mirror spoke in its cool, clear voice.

"The Mirror of Dreams showed Cordelia her heart's desire, and
her heart desires a true friend and companion – someone who is
not jealous of her wealth, but a friend who will share her hopes and
dreams, and with whom she can have parties, games and picnics."

Polly put the mirror down and thought with amazement
that she could be that friend, if Cordelia would be friends with
someone poor but honest and true. Polly left the mirror with the
household rubbish and was about to make the descent back to
the basement, when she saw Cordelia standing in the garden at
the back of the house. Cordelia had seen her discard the mirror
and shyly walked up to Polly. Polly overcame her shyness, too,
and went to meet Cordelia and then she told her they shared the
same dream.

Cordelia and Polly became the best of friends from that day on.
They shared everything they had, no matter how much or little.
They talked and laughed together all day long and they played long
into the evening. They didn't have to dream any more, for they
had both got their true heart's desire.

Mr Mole Gets Lost

Mr Mole poked his little black nose out from the top of one of his molehills and had a great big sniff of the air. Then, he sniffed again. And then, a third time just to make sure. "Oh dear," he thought, "it smells like it's going to rain."

Mr Mole didn't like the rain one bit. Every time he got caught in the rain his plush little velvet fur coat got all wet and drippy and he left muddy footprints all over his underground burrow. But worse still, the rain got in through the holes in his molehills and then everything got all soggy and took days to dry out.

Well, the skies got darker and darker and very soon little spots of rain began to fall. Then, the spots became bigger. And then, bigger still. Before long, all you could see before your eyes were big, straight rods of rain bouncing off the leaves on the trees, pounding the ground and turning everything muddy and wet.

Mr Mole had never seen rain like it. He sat in his burrow in the middle of the meadow wishing it would stop. But it just kept raining and raining. Soon, the rain started entering his burrow. First, it went drip, drip, drip through the holes in his molehills and then it became a little river of water in the bottom of his burrow. Then, the little river became a bigger, faster-flowing river and suddenly Mr Mole was being washed along by it. Through the tunnels of his burrow he went, this way and then that, as the water gushed and poured through his underground home.

The next thing he knew he was being washed out of his burrow completely, as the rain water carried him off down the meadow. Down he went, not knowing which way up he was or where he was going. Now, he was being washed through the woods at the bottom of the meadow, but still the water carried him on, bouncing and turning him until he was dizzy and gasping for breath.

Suddenly, he came to a halt. The rain water gurgled and trickled around him and then flowed onwards, as he found himself stuck firmly in the branches of a bush. "Oh dear," Mr Mole said as he got himself free. "Goodness me, where can I be?" he thought. Mr Mole looked around him, but being a very short-sighted mole – as most moles are – he couldn't make out any of the places that were familiar to him. Worse still, he couldn't smell any smells that were familiar to him. He was completely lost, far from home, and had no idea how to get back again. Now, to make things worse, it was starting to get dark.

"Woo-oo-oo-oo-oo!" said a voice suddenly. Mr Mole nearly jumped out of his moleskin with fright. "I wouldn't stay here if I were you," said the voice again. Mr Mole looked up and found himself face to face with an enormous owl. "Don't you know it's not safe in the woods at night?" asked the owl. "There are snakes and foxes and weasels and all sorts of nasty creatures that you really wouldn't like to meet."

"Oh dear!" was all Mr Mole could think of saying. He told the owl of his terrible watery journey and how he was lost and didn't know how to get back home again.

"You need to talk to Polly Pigeon," said the owl. "She is a homing pigeon and she lives near your meadow. She can show you the way home. But we'll have to find her first. Stay close to me, mind, and look out for those snakes, foxes and weasels I told you about."

Mr Mole didn't need telling twice. He stayed so close to the
kindly owl that every time the owl stopped or turned round to
talk to Mr Mole, Mr Mole bumped right into him!

Through the dark, dangerous woods they went. Every now and
again, there would be an unfriendly noise, such as a deep growl or
a hiss, coming from the dense, tangled trees, but Mr Mole didn't
want to think about that too much, so he just made sure that he
never lost sight of the owl.

Finally, just when Mr Mole thought that he couldn't go a step
further, they came to a halt by an old elm tree.

"Hallo-oooo," called the owl.

They were in luck. Polly Pigeon was waking up and they found
her just in time for she was about to continue her journey home.

"Please," said Mr Mole, "I'm afraid I'm terribly lost and don't know how to get back to my meadow. Will you take me there?"

"Of course I will," said Polly Pigeon. "We'd better let you rest here a while first, though. But we must go before it gets light."

So Mr Mole was soon trudging wearily back to his meadow, following as closely behind Polly Pigeon as he was able. Just as the first rays of Sun lit the morning sky, Mr Mole smelled a very familiar smell. It was his meadow! He was almost home!

Soon, he was back in his own burrow. It was so wet and muddy, however, that the first thing he did was build some new tunnels higher up the meadow so that the rain wouldn't wash down into them so easily. Then, he settled down to eat one of his supplies of worms and fell into a deep, well-earned slumber.

The Wolf and the Seven Goats

There was once an old mother goat who had seven little goats.
They all lived in a tiny house on the edge of a big, dark forest.
One day, the mother goat had to go into the forest to collect food.
Before she left, she called her seven little goats to her and said,
"Now, children, promise me that while I am away you will lock
the door and be on your guard against the wicked wolf. If you see
him, don't let him in, because he would certainly eat you all up.
You can recognize him by his gruff voice and his big black paws."

"Yes, mother," the little goats replied, "we promise to be
very careful."

So the mother goat trotted cheerfully away into the forest and the little goats locked the door. Some time later, there was a knock at the door and the little goats heard a voice calling, "Open the door, children, it is your mother. I have brought back a present for each of you."

But the little goats heard that the voice was gruff, and not the gentle voice of their mother and so they called, "No, we will not let you in! You do not have a soft voice like our mother's, you have a gruff voice. You are the wolf!"

So the cunning wolf went to a shop and stole a jar of syrup and swallowed it to make his voice soft. Then, back he went to the little house by the forest. "Open the door, children," he called in his new, soft voice. "It is your mother. I have brought back a present for each of you."

Now, the little goats heard the soft voice, but in his eagerness to get into the house the wolf had put his big black paws on to the window ledge, and so the little goats cried out, "No, we will not let you in! Our mother has beautiful white feet, but you have black feet. You are the wolf!"

So the wolf ran back into the village and went to the baker's shop, where he stole some flour and covered his paws in it. The wolf ran back to the little house by the forest. "Children, children, open the door!" he called again. "It is your mother. I have brought back a present for each of you."

The little goats heard the soft voice but they could not see any paws and they called out, "Let us see your paws so that we know you really are our mother." So the wolf lifted up his paws, which of course were all white from the flour plastered on them. The little goats thought that this time it really was their mother and they unlocked the door.

The wolf rushed in. The little goats screamed and tried to
hide. One jumped into a drawer; the second squeezed under the
bed; the third buried itself in the bedclothes; the fourth leaped
into a cupboard; the fifth went into the oven; the sixth hid
under a basin; and the littlest one slipped inside the grandfather
clock. But the wolf found them and gobbled them up – all except
the youngest one hiding in the grandfather clock. When the
wolf had finished his meal, he felt very full and very sleepy. He
wandered out of the house into a nearby meadow, lay down on
some dry leaves and promptly fell asleep.

When the mother goat came home from the forest, imagine her horror as she saw the door open, the furniture strewn around the house and the little goats all gone. She started calling them by name, but nobody answered until she called out the name of the youngest little goat, who was still hiding in the grandfather clock. She quickly pulled him out and then he told her what had happened to all his brothers and sisters.

She ran out of the house with the little goat trotting beside her and soon found the wolf sleeping in the meadow. She looked carefully at him and saw that there were six lumps in his fat stomach and that they seemed to be moving. "My little goats are still alive," she exclaimed with joy.

Quickly, she sent the youngest goat back to her house for scissors, needle and thread. Then, while the wolf was still sleeping, she carefully cut a hole in the wolf's stomach. Soon, a little goat popped out and then another and another, until all six were free and jumping for joy. They had not come to any harm, for in his greed the wolf had swallowed them all whole.

"Quick," cried the mother goat, "fetch me some rocks from the river so that I can fill up this wicked wolf's stomach." So the little goats each fetched a rock and the mother goat sewed them up inside the wolf's stomach.

When the wolf awoke, he was very thirsty. "What is the matter with me?" he thought. "I shouldn't have eaten all those goats at once. Now I've got indigestion." He set out to drink from the river. But his stomach was so heavy he could hardly walk and he staggered to the water's edge. As he bent over to drink, the weight of the stones pulled the wolf into the water, and he was never seen again. Then, the mother goat and all her little goats – who had been watching – danced for joy. For never again would they be afraid of the wicked wolf!

The Runaway Train

Once upon a time, there was a little kingdom in a far-off place. Although the people in the kingdom were ruled by a kindly king, the kingdom was mountainous and barren and many of the people were very poor.

Each month, there was a market. Market day was a very important day for all the villagers in the kingdom, just as it is for people everywhere.

The market was held in a big, broad valley nestling among the snowy peaks and people made their way to it from far and wide to sell their crops, or to buy new clothes or things for their homes.

People living up in the mountains would take the mountain passes and walk down into the valley. Those living a little further down the mountain would saddle up their donkeys and mules and ride to the market. But for people living at the bottom of the mountains, the best way to get to the market was to take the old steam train. The train ran from the bottom of the mountains all the way up to the top and then down into the valley.

One day, a poor farmer who lived at the bottom of the mountains woke up and went to harvest the crops on his small farm. But the crop was poor. There was barely enough food to make a meal for his family and himself.

The poor farmer wondered what he could sell at the market, in order that his family and himself might have enough food to eat. He had no crops to sell and he had already sold almost everything else he could spare. The only thing he had left to sell was his cockatoo.

The thought of selling his cockatoo filled him with great sadness. The cockatoo was a fine-looking bird, with colourful ivory, red and yellow feathers. Not only was it fine-looking, but it was thought by everyone to be a very clever bird, too. It seemed to understand whatever you said and was a great favourite with all the family.

The farmer looked at his hungry family and then he looked at the cockatoo. The cockatoo looked back at the farmer as if it understood what the farmer was thinking.

"I must sell the cockatoo at the market," said the farmer, finally. "We have no crops to eat and we must buy food. There is nothing else we can sell to raise the money we need."

On the very next market day, the farmer climbed aboard the train for its journey up the mountains and down into the valley to the market. In his hand, he held a little metal cage and sitting in the cage, looking very sad, was his beloved cockatoo.

The old train collected more people from the villages and then began its long, steep journey up the mountains. It chuffed and puffed, and puffed and chuffed, but then suddenly, with a bang, a clang and a groan, it came to a halt. The boiler on the old train had exploded! Then, slowly, the train started to roll back down the mountain slope. The driver tried the brakes, but it was no use. The old train just carried on rolling backwards, gathering speed all the time.

Everyone on board was very frightened, for there was nothing to stop the train hurtling all the way down the track and overturning at the bottom of the mountains.

Suddenly, the farmer had an idea. He lifted the cockatoo's cage close to his head and spoke to the cockatoo. "Fly down the mountain, as fast as you can, and raise the alarm!" he said. Then, he opened the cockatoo's cage and released the bird.

Down the mountain the cockatoo flew as fast as its wings could take it. Straight to the railway station it went and landed on the steps of the stationmaster's office.

"Hello, what are you doing here?" said the stationmaster, for he recognized the cockatoo by its bright, colourful feathers.

The cockatoo flew into the air and hovered in front of the stationmaster, then it flew out of his office. Then, it flew back into the office, flapped its wings in front of the stationmaster and flew out again.

"Well, I do believe you want me to follow you," said the stationmaster. So he went outside.

Suddenly, something made the stationmaster look up towards the mountain and he saw the runaway train. "Quick!" he called to his station guards. "Bring some sand and follow me!" The stationmaster and the guards quickly loaded sacks of sand. Then, they threw it on to the track. Backwards and forwards they went with their sacks of sand, until a great mound of sand lay across the track, right in the path of the runaway train.

Suddenly, the runaway train came into sight, clanking and rumbling helplessly down the track. Then, it hit the heap of sand on the track and, amid more rumbling and grinding, it came to a safe halt.

Shaken, but safe, the passengers climbed out of the carriages. The stationmaster explained what had happened and how the cockatoo had helped stop the runaway train.

"How could I ever have thought of selling you, my friend," said the farmer to his cockatoo. "From now on, we will always keep you safely."

All the villagers were so grateful to the farmer and his cockatoo, that they all gave some of their crops to help feed the farmer and his family until his own crops grew again.

Little Tim and His Brother Sam

Little Tim was a very lucky boy. He had a lovely home, with the nicest parents you could hope for. He had a big garden, with a swing and a football net in it. And growing in the garden were lots of trees that you could climb and have adventures in. Little Tim even had a nice school, which he enjoyed going to every day and where he had lots of friends. In fact, almost everything in Tim's life was nice. Everything that is apart from one thing – Tim's brother, Sam.

Sam was a very naughty boy. Worse still, whenever he got into mischief – which he did almost all of the time – he managed to make it look as though someone else was to blame. And that someone was usually poor Tim!

Once, Sam thought that he would put salt in the sugar bowl instead of sugar. That afternoon, Sam and Tim's parents had some friends round for tea. All the guests put salt in their cups of tea, of course, thinking it was sugar. Well, being very polite they didn't like to say anything, even though their cups of tea tasted very strange indeed! When Sam and Tim's parents tasted their tea, however, they guessed immediately that someone had been playing a trick. They had to apologize to their guests and make them all fresh cups of tea. And who got the blame? Little Tim did, because Sam had sprinkled salt on Tim's bedroom floor so that their mother would think that Tim was the culprit.

Another time, Sam and Tim were playing football in the garden when Sam accidentally kicked the ball against a window and broke it. Sam immediately ran away and hid, so that when their father came out to investigate, only Tim was to be seen. So poor little Tim got the blame again.

Then, there was the time when Sam and Tim's Aunt Jessica
came to stay. She was a very nice lady, but she hated anything
creepy-crawly, and as far as she was concerned that included
frogs. So what did Sam do? Why, he went down to the garden
pond and got a big, green frog to put in Aunt Jessica's handbag.
When Aunt Jessica opened her handbag to get her glasses out,
there staring out of the bag at her were two froggy eyes.

"Croak!" said the frog.

"Eeek!" yelled Aunt Jessica and almost jumped out of her skin.

"I told Tim not to do it," said Sam.

Tim opened his mouth and was just about to protest his
innocence when his mother said, "Tim, go to your room
immediately and don't come out until you are told."

Poor Tim went to his room and had to stay there until after supper. Sam thought it was very funny.

The next day, Sam decided that he would play another prank and blame it on Tim. He went to the garden shed and, one by one, took out all the garden tools. When he thought no one was watching, he hid them all in Tim's bedroom cupboard. In went the spade, the fork, the watering can, the trowel – in fact, everything except the lawnmower. And the only reason that the lawnmower didn't go in was because it was too heavy to carry!

But this time, Sam's little prank was about to come unstuck, for Aunt Jessica had seen him creeping up the stairs to Tim's bedroom with the garden tools. She guessed immediately what Sam was up to and who was likely to get the blame. When Sam wasn't about, she spoke to Tim. The two of them whispered to each other for a few seconds and then smiled triumphantly.

Later that day, Sam and Tim's father went to the garden shed to do some gardening. Imagine his surprise when all he saw were some old flower pots and the lawnmower. He searched high and low for the garden tools. He looked behind the compost heap, under the garden steps, behind the sand pit and in the garage. But they weren't anywhere to be seen.

Then, he started searching in the house. He looked in the kitchen cupboard and was just looking under the stairs when something at the top of the stairs caught his eye. The handle from the garden spade was sticking out of the door to Sam's bedroom. Looking rather puzzled, he went upstairs and walked into Sam's bedroom. There, nestling neatly in the cupboard, were the rest of the tools.

"Sam, come up here immediately," called his father.

Sam, not realizing anything was amiss, came sauntering upstairs. Suddenly, he saw all the garden tools that he had so carefully hidden in Tim's cupboard now sitting in *his* cupboard. He was speechless.

"Right," said his father, "before you go out to play, you can take all the tools back down to the garden shed. Then you can cut the grass. Then you can dig over the flower beds and then you can do the weeding."

Well, it took Sam hours to do all the gardening. Tim and Aunt Jessica watched from the window and clutched their sides with laughter. Sam never did find out how all the garden tools found their way into his bedroom, but I think you've guessed, haven't you?

The Dragon Who
Was Scared of Flying

Once upon a time, in a land far away, there lived a dragon named Dennis. He lived in a cave high up in the mountains. All his friends lived in caves nearby and his own brothers and sisters lived right next door. Now, you would think that Dennis would have been a very happy dragon, surrounded by his friends and family, wouldn't you? Well, I'm sorry to say that Dennis was, in fact, a very unhappy and lonely dragon.

The reason for this was that Dennis was scared of flying. Every day, his friends would set off to have adventures, leaving poor Dennis behind on his own. Dennis would stare out of his cave at the departing dragons. How he wished he could join them!

After they had gone, he would stand on the ledge outside his cave, trying to build up the courage to fly. But as soon as he looked over the edge, he felt all giddy and had to step back. Then, he would crawl back into his cave defeated and spend the rest of the day counting stalactites on the ceiling or rearranging his collection of bat bones.

Every evening, the other dragons would return with amazing tales of what they had been up to that day. "I rescued a damsel in distress," one would say.

"I fought the wicked one-eyed giant and won," boasted another.

"I helped light the fire for a witch's cauldron," announced a third.

"What have you been up to?" Dennis' sister Doreen used to ask him.

"Oh … um … this and that," Dennis would reply mournfully, looking down at his scaly toes. Then, Doreen would lead him out of the cave and try to teach him to fly. Dennis would take a running jump and flap his wings furiously but his feet would stay firmly on the ground. Then, the other dragons would laugh so much that, in the end, he always gave up.

One day, Dennis could stand it no longer. The other dragons flew off as usual to find adventure but Dennis, instead of retreating into his cave, set off down the mountainside. It was very tiring having to walk. Dennis had never really been further than from his cave to the ledge and back, and soon he was puffing and panting. He was about to rest at the side of the path when his eye was caught by something colourful in the distance. Down in the valley he could make out some brightly coloured tents and now he could hear the faint strains of music drifting up to him. "I'd better take a closer look," thought Dennis. "Maybe I can have an adventure, like the other dragons!" He got so excited at the thought of his very own adventure that he started to run. Then, he got all out of breath and had to stop altogether for a while.

At last, Dennis reached the tents and found himself in a world more exotic than he could ever have imagined. He was surrounded by strange, four-legged creatures, such as he had never seen before. There was a yellow creature that roared and another one with stripes and fierce teeth. There were also quite a few hairy creatures with long tails. These ones were dressed up to look like boys and girls. Can you guess what all these creatures were? Of course, Dennis had never seen a lion or a tiger or a chimpanzee before. He thought they were very peculiar! The animals thought Dennis was very odd, too. They stood in a circle around him. "How strange," snarled the lion. "A slimy thing with wings!"

"It doesn't look very fit!" growled the tiger, flexing his claws.

"Look at its funny, knobbly tail," giggled the chimpanzees.

Dennis began to feel unhappy and unwanted again, but at that moment he heard a friendly voice saying, "Hello, there! Welcome to Chippy's Circus. I'm Claude the clown. How do you do?"

Dennis turned round. Now, he felt really confused, for standing behind him was a man with the unhappiest face Dennis had ever seen. He had great sad eyes and a mouth that was turned down so far that it seemed to touch his chin. Yet he spoke so cheerfully!

"I'm Dennis the dragon," said Dennis.

"A dragon, eh?" said Claude. "Well, we've never had a dragon in the circus before. Might be quite a crowd puller! Would you like to join the circus?" he asked.

"Oh, yes please," cried Dennis.

"Very well," said Claude. "I'm sure you're very talented," he added.

So Dennis joined the circus and was happy for the first time in his life. The other animals became quite friendly now that they knew what he was. Claude taught Dennis to ride the unicycle and to do acrobatic tricks. He also learned how to dive into a bucket of water. He didn't mind that a bit because his slimy skin was quite waterproof! Now, as you know, dragons are particularly

330

good at breathing fire, so Dennis soon became the circus' champion fire-eater. People would come from far and near to see Dennis shooting flames high into the dark roof of the big top.

One evening, Dennis had just finished his fire-eating act. He was eating an ice cream to cool his hot throat and watching Carlotta, the tightrope walker. She was pirouetting high up on the rope as usual. Then all at once, she lost her footing and Dennis saw to his horror that she was going to fall. He dropped his ice cream and, without thinking, flapped his wings furiously. As Carlotta fell, Dennis found himself flying up towards her. He caught her gently on his back and flew down to the ground with her clinging on tightly. The crowd roared and burst into applause. They obviously thought it was all part of the act.

"Thank you, Dennis," whispered Carlotta in Dennis' ear. "You saved my life."

Dennis was overjoyed. Not only had he saved Carlotta's life, he had also learned to fly. And he said with a grin, "I do declare that flying is actually rather fun."

331

The Mean King and the Crafty Lad

There was once a king who was as mean as he was rich. He lived in a great palace where he spent his days counting his bags of gold coins. Meanwhile, his subjects lived in great poverty. Sometimes, the King would summon his page to prepare the royal carriage. Then, the King would set forth in his great, golden coach to survey his kingdom.

Now, not only was the King extremely rich, but he was very vain. As he passed his subjects working in the field, he liked them to bow to him and pay him compliments. "How handsome you look today, Your Majesty!" they would call, or "How well the colour pink suits you, Sire!"

His head would swell with pride as he moved on. "My people truly adore me!" he would say.

But for all their complimentary words, the people hated their King. They resented the fact that the King lived in splendour while his subjects toiled hard all their lives. At last, a secret meeting was called among the peasants. "Let's sign a petition demanding our rights!" cried one man.

"And fair pay!" shouted another. They all cheered and clapped their hands.

"Who's going to write down our demands?" called an old woman. Now, the crowd was hushed, for none of them knew how to read or write.

"I know what we can do instead," called a voice from the back. Everyone turned round to see a young lad in rags. "Let's march on the palace!" he cried.

"Yes!" roared the crowd.

As the angry mob reached the palace, the King saw them and sent out his guard dogs. The peasants were forced to flee for their lives with the dogs snapping at their ankles. Not until the last peasant was out of sight did the King call off his dogs. "Good work!" he cried.

From then on, however, life became even harder for the people because the King was on his guard in case they marched on the castle again. Now, when he went out and about in his kingdom, he was always accompanied by his hounds.

Eventually, another secret meeting was called. "What can we do?" the people said. "We will never be able to get past those savage dogs."

"I've got an idea," came a familiar voice. It was the ragged lad again. For a while, there was uproar as people accused him of having nearly lost them their lives. "Please trust me," pleaded the lad. "I know I let you down, but this time I've got a well thought-out plan to get the King to give up his money." In the end, the peasants listened to the boy's scheme and decided to let him try.

The next day, the boy hid in a branch of a tree that overhung the palace garden. With him he had some dog biscuits, in which he had hidden a powerful sleeping pill. He threw the biscuits on

to the palace lawn and waited. Some
time later, as the boy had hoped,
the king's hounds came out on
to the lawn. They headed straight
for the biscuits and gobbled them up.
Soon, they were fast asleep, one and all. Quickly, the lad
slid out of the tree and, donning a large black cape, he ran
round to the front of the palace and rapped on the door.

A sentry opened the door. "Good day," said the lad, "I
am Victor, the world-famous vet. Do you have any
animals requiring medical attention?"

"No," replied the sentry, slamming the door in the
lad's face. Just then, voices could be heard from within the palace.
After a few moments, the sentry opened the door again and said,
"As a matter of fact, we do have a bit of a problem. Step inside."

The sentry led the lad out to the lawn where the
King was weeping over the dogs' bodies. "Oh, please
help," he cried. "I need my dogs. Without them
I may be besieged by my
own people."

The lad pretended to examine the dogs. He said to the King, "I have only seen one case like this before. The only cure is to feed the animals liquid gold."

"Liquid gold?" exclaimed the King. "Wherever shall I find liquid gold?"

"Fear not," said the lad, "I have a friend – a witch – who lives in the mountains. She can turn gold coins into liquid gold. You must let me take the dogs – and a bag of gold – to her and she will cure them."

Well, the King was so beside himself with fear that he readily agreed. The sleeping dogs were loaded on to a horse-drawn cart and the King gave the lad a bag of gold saying, "Hurry back, my dogs are most precious."

Off went the lad, back to his home. His mother and father helped him unload the dogs, who by now were beginning to wake up. They took great care of the dogs, who were glad to be looked after kindly for once. The next day, the lad put on the cloak again

336

and returned to the palace. "The good news is," he said to the King, "that the cure is working. The bad news is that there was only enough gold to revive one dog. I'll need all the gold you've got to cure the others."

"Take it all," screamed the King, "only I must have my dogs back tomorrow!" He opened the safe and threw his entire stock of gold on to another cart, which the young lad dragged away.

That night, the lad gave each of the king's subjects a bag of gold. The next morning, he led the dogs back to the palace. To his surprise, the King didn't want them back. "Now I have no gold," he said, "I don't need guard dogs."

Then, the lad saw that the King had learned his lesson and he told the King what had really happened. And to everyone's joy, the King said the peasants could keep their bags of gold. As for the King, he kept the dogs as pets and became a much nicer person.

No Hunting!

Mr Rabbit opened his eyes and gave a big yawn. He thought it seemed like the perfect day for going outside and nibbling some of the farmer's lettuces. And after that he thought he would go and see how well the farmer's carrots were growing and maybe have a little nibble of those as well. He popped his head out of his burrow and looked this way and that, in case he saw any danger. Then, he pricked up his ears and turned this way and that, in case he heard any danger. Finally, he sniffed the air this way and that, in case he smelled any danger. It seemed safe, so he hopped out of his burrow.

No sooner had he gone a couple of steps when "ZING" – a bullet whizzed past his head. Mr Rabbit jumped back into his burrow as fast as he could go, shaking with fright.

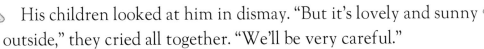

"Goodness, it's the rabbit hunting season," he gasped. He gathered his family of young rabbits around him and spoke to them. "Now children, listen very carefully," he said. "The rabbit hunting season has begun, so you must all stay safely inside the burrow until it's over. I will go out at night and forage for food for us all."

His children looked at him in dismay. "But it's lovely and sunny outside," they cried all together. "We'll be very careful."

But Mr Rabbit was having none of it. He insisted that they all stay underground until the rabbit season was over.

For a few days, the young rabbits amused themselves as best they could by playing chase and hide and seek. But they were becoming very bored. Finally, they decided that they were going to do something to stop the rabbit hunting themselves.

First, Tom, the eldest of Mr Rabbit's children, decided he would try and stop the hunters. So when it was dark, he crept out of the burrow and made his way towards the hunters' hut.

Although it was night and he was sure the hunters would be asleep, he was still very scared. Soon, he came to the hut. It was standing in a clearing in the woods. It was dark inside the hut and he hoped the hunters were asleep. "If I can dig some big holes," he thought, "maybe they will fall into them in the morning and won't be able to get out until the hunting season is over."

So he dug and he dug like he had never dug before. Soon, there were holes everywhere, right outside the door to the hunters' hut. Feeling very pleased with himself, but also very tired, Tom made his way back to the burrow just before it was light.

When the hunters awoke, they went straight out without falling down a single hole! Poor Tom, he had dug lots of holes alright, but the hunters' hut had two doors and the hunters had simply gone out of the other one!

340

NO HUNTING!

Then Jenny, the second eldest of Mr Rabbit's children, decided that she would try and stop the hunters. So when it was dark, she crept out of the burrow and made her way towards the hunters' hut. When she got there, she noticed that the window was open and so she decided to go inside. She, too, was very scared, but she thought about having to spend all those days in the burrow until the hunting season was over and that gave her the courage to carry on.

Inside the hut, she could see the hunters sleeping in their beds. She looked around, wondering what she could do to stop them hunting. Then suddenly, she saw the hunters' clothes lying on a chair. Quick as a flash, she hopped up to them and started nibbling at them. In no time at all, the clothes were in shreds.

"That'll stop them," thought Jenny. "They can't hunt without their clothes on!" Satisfied with her night's work, Jenny made her way back to the burrow just as dawn was breaking.

When the hunters awoke, they got straight up and went out hunting! Poor Jenny, she had chewed some clothes alright, but she had only chewed some spare clothes! The hunters had gone to bed wearing their other clothes in order to be out quickly in the morning.

Finally, Penelope, the youngest of Mr Rabbit's children, said she would try and stop the hunters.

"Don't be silly," said Tom to his sister. "You are far too young to be going out at night."

"And anyway," said Jenny, "what could you possibly think of doing to stop the hunters?"

"I'll think of something," said Penelope, who was really quite a clever little rabbit.

So that night, she crept out of the burrow and made her way to the hunters' hut. The window was open, just as before, and so Penelope hopped inside. She looked on the floor, she looked in the cupboards and she looked under the beds, but she couldn't think of anything to stop the hunters.

Then, she looked up and suddenly had an idea. For there on the table was a calendar, showing that very day's date. Penelope hopped on to the table and started to turn the pages. Finally, she came to a page on the calendar that read: "Rabbit hunting season ends today". Satisfied with her work, Penelope hopped out of the hunters' hut and back home to her burrow.

In the morning, the hunters woke up, rubbed their eyes and got out of their beds. One of them glanced at the calendar. "Oh no!" he suddenly exclaimed. "Look at the date! The rabbit hunting season is over."

With that, the hunters (who were too silly to realize that someone else must have turned over the pages of the calendar) packed their belongings and went home. All was peace and quiet once more and the rabbits could hop about in the open air in safety.

Puss in Boots

Once upon a time in France, there lived a miller who had three sons. When he died, the miller left the mill to his eldest son. To his second son he left a donkey on whose back sacks of flour could be loaded and delivered to customers. But to the youngest son, who was much the most handsome of the three, he left only a large cat, whose job it had been to chase the mice that came at night to make holes in the sacks and steal grain.

The poor youngest brother wondered how on earth he would make his living with only the cat for company. He could see that he would have to go out into the world to seek his fortune. "I shall have to leave you behind, Puss," he said, "for I don't see how I am to look after you."

"What about if I looked after *you?*" replied Puss.

"Whatever do you mean?" said his master.

"I can make your fortune for you," said the cat. "All I need is a good-sized drawstring bag and a pair of really nice boots – for my hind feet."

Well, the lad was mightily puzzled, but he decided it was worth letting the cat try to win his fortune, as he surely had no idea of what to do otherwise. With his brand new boots on his hind paws and his drawstring bag slung over his shoulder, Puss set off with nothing but a handful of corn from the mill.

The first thing he did was go straight to the nearest rabbit warren where he opened the bag, put a little corn into it and laid it open near the rabbit hole. Then, Puss laid in wait until dusk, when the rabbits came out of their hole. One rabbit came up, full of curiosity, and hopped into the bag to get the corn. Up sprang Puss and pulled the drawstring tight. Then, instead of taking the rabbit to his master, he set off to the palace, where he announced that he had brought the King a present.

"Your Majesty," said Puss, taking a low bow, "I am a messenger from the Marquis of Carabas, your neighbour. He was out hunting today and was lucky enough to catch a fine young rabbit. He begs that you will accept it as a present."

The King was puzzled, because he'd never heard of this Marquis, but he was pleased to have the rabbit. "Tell your master that I am delighted with his kind present," he said.

Day after day, Puss went out hunting in this manner and each time he presented his catch to the King. "Don't forget," he said to his master, "that you're supposed to be a Marquis." The young boy had no idea what the cat was talking about, but he trusted him nevertheless. After a while the cat started to be invited in for a drink and a chat with the guards and he soon got to know all the court gossip. One time, Puss got to hear that the King was planning to ride the next day in his grand carriage with his daughter, the most beautiful princess in France. Puss took care to find out which direction they intended to take.

The next morning, he said to his master, "I think it would be a good idea to take a swim in the river this morning." The lad agreed and, by the look in Puss' eye, he knew that he had a plan in mind. Puss led the way to a part of the river where the royal carriage was bound to pass. While the boy was swimming in the river, Puss heard the sound of the approaching carriage. Quickly, Puss hid his master's ragged clothes under a stone and as the carriage came into view he ran into the road shouting, "Help! The Marquis of Carabas is drowning!" At once, the King recognized Puss and ordered his guards to go to the rescue. The lad pretended to be drowning, so that the guards had quite a struggle to get him to the bank.

Meanwhile, Puss went up to the carriage, bowed to the King and said, "While he was bathing, thieves unfortunately stole my master's fine clothing. He cannot appear before your daughter without any clothes."

"Of course not," replied the King and sent his footman to fetch a spare set of clothes from the back of the royal carriage. Now, that the handsome lad was properly dressed, the King was glad to meet the mysterious Marquis, of whom he had heard so much from Puss. He welcomed the 'Marquis' into the carriage, where he sat next to the Princess. "Come for a drive with us, my dear Marquis," said the King.

Without another word Puss set off and disappeared around the next bend of the road. By the time the King's gilded carriage was on its way again, Puss was a long way ahead. Soon, he passed a field of haymakers. "My good haymakers," said Puss, "you must tell the King that this meadow belongs to the Marquis of Carabas – or I'll grind you all to little pieces."

Now, Puss knew that the meadow really belonged to an ogre, who was known to be able to change his shape. So of course the haymakers had no idea if this was just an ordinary pussy cat telling them what to do – or if it really was the ogre. Soon, the royal carriage passed by and the King leaned out and asked to whom the field belonged. "To the Marquis of Carabas, Your Majesty," chorused the haymakers.

"That's a fine piece of land you've got there," said the King, nudging the lad who was busy chatting to the Princess.

All along the road it was the same story. Puss always got there before the royal carriage. Woodcutters, shepherds and farmers all told the King that their master was the Marquis of Carabas, because Puss had threatened to turn them all into mincemeat if they didn't. Now, Puss caught sight of a fine castle which he recognized as belonging to the ogre.

Puss went up to the great gate and asked to speak to the ogre. Puss said to him, "I heard that you can transform yourself in the most amazing way – into a lion for example. But I really can't believe that this is true."

The ogre was so offended that he bellowed, "JUST YOU WATCH!" and instantly turned himself into a lion. Puss pretended to be scared and jumped up on to the castle roof. The ogre turned himself back into an ogre. "That'll teach you," he roared.

"You gave me a dreadful fright," said Puss. "Do you know, people say you can even turn yourself into a tiny animal, such as rat or mouse. But that's absurd. It's quite impossible."

"IMPOSSIBLE, EH?" screeched the ogre and the great foolish creature turned himself into a mouse.

In an instant, Puss had pounced on him and gobbled him up, bones and all. At that moment, the royal carriage rumbled over the drawbridge, for the King, too, had spotted the castle and wondered who lived there.

"Welcome to the castle of the Marquis of Carabas, Your Majesty," said Puss, who had just wiped the last morsels of the ogre from his whiskers.

"What," cried the King, turning to the young boy, "is this yours, too?" The lad glanced at Puss and then nodded. "May we see inside?" went on the King.

So the King, the Princess and the miller's son looked around the castle. And very fine it was, too. The ogre's servants were so happy to see the back of their master that they laid on a fine feast. And at the end of the meal, the King agreed to give his daughter's hand in marriage to the 'Marquis'.

As for Puss, his master was so grateful that he saw to it that the cat was made a lord. So they all lived happily ever after and Puss never had to chase another mouse for the rest of his life.

 # The Golden Bird

There was once a king who kept a golden bird in a gilded cage. The bird wanted for nothing. Every day, the king's servant brought him food and water and groomed his fine yellow feathers. And each day, the bird sang his beautiful song for the King. "How lucky I am," cried the King, "to have such a beautiful bird that sings such a fine song." However, as time passed the King began to feel sorry for the bird. "It really isn't fair," he thought, "to keep such a handsome creature in a cage. I must give the bird its freedom." He called his servant and ordered him to take the cage into the jungle and release the bird.

The servant obeyed and took the cage deep into the jungle where he came to a small clearing. He set the cage down, opened the door and out hopped the golden bird. "I hope you can look after yourself," the servant said as he walked away.

The golden bird looked about him. "This is strange!" he thought to himself. "Still, I suppose someone will come along to feed me soon." He settled down and waited.

After a while, he heard a crashing sound in the trees and then he saw a monkey swinging from branch to branch on his long arms.

"Hello there!" called the monkey, hanging by his tail and casting the bird an upside down grin. "Who are you?"

"I am the golden bird," replied the golden bird haughtily.

"I can see you're new around here," said the monkey. "I'll show you the best places to feed in the tree tops."

"No thanks," replied the golden bird ungratefully. "What could an ape like you possibly teach me? You've got such a funny face. I expect you're envious of my beautiful beak," he added. "Have it your own way," called the monkey as he swung off into the trees.

Some time later, the golden bird heard a hissing noise in the undergrowth and a snake came slithering by. "Well, hello," hissed the snake. "Who are you?"

"I am the golden bird," replied the golden bird proudly.

"Let me show you the jungle paths," said the snake.

"No thanks," replied the bird rudely. "What could a snake possibly teach me? With your horrid hissing voice, you must be jealous of my beautiful song," he said, forgetting that he had not opened his beak to sing yet.

"Very well," hissed the snake as he slithered away into the undergrowth.

By now, the golden bird was beginning to wonder when his food would arrive. He began to imagine the tasty morsel that he hoped he would soon be eating. Just then, he was aware of a movement on the tree trunk behind him. Looking up he caught a glimpse of a chameleon, lying camouflaged against the trunk.

"Good day," said the chameleon. "I've been here all the time, so I know who you are. You're the golden bird. I've heard you say it twice. It's a good idea to know where to hide in case of danger. Let me show you."

"No thanks," replied the golden bird. "What could an ugly brute like you possibly teach me? You must wish you had lovely feathers like me," he said, fluffing up his beautiful, golden plumage.

"Don't say I didn't warn you," muttered the chameleon as he darted away.

355

The golden bird had just settled down again when a great grey shadow passed over the jungle. He looked up to see an eagle swooping low over the trees. The monkey swung up to hide in the densest foliage near the top of the trees. The snake slid into the deepest part of the undergrowth. The chameleon stayed quite still but his skin colour became a perfect match for the tree he was on and he became totally invisible.

"Aha!" thought the golden bird. "All I have to do is fly away and that stupid eagle will never catch up with me." He flapped his wings and flapped and flapped, but he did not know that his wings had grown weak through living a life of luxury in the palace. Now, the bird regretted his golden plumage and wished that he had dull brown feathers that would not show up in the forest clearing. For his fine yellow feathers made him easy to see. He was sure the eagle would come and gobble him up. "Help!" he trilled. "Please help me someone." Now he could see the eagle swooping down towards him with eyes blazing like fire and talons drawn.

At that moment, the golden bird felt something close around his legs and pull him into the undergrowth. It was the snake. Then, he was lifted up into the trees by a long, hairy arm and saw he was being carried by the monkey. "Keep still," whispered the chameleon pushing him into the centre of a large yellow flower. "The eagle won't see you there." And sure enough, the golden bird found that he was precisely the colour of the flower and the eagle flew straight past him.

"However can I repay you all?" exclaimed the bird. "You saved my life!"

"You can sing for us," replied the animals. And from then on, the monkey, the snake and the chameleon looked after the golden bird and he sang his beautiful song for them every day.

The Boy Who Wished Too Much

There once was a young boy named Billy. He was a lucky lad, for he had parents who loved him, plenty of friends and a room full of toys. Behind his house was a rubbish tip. Billy had been forbidden to go there by his mother, but he used to stare at it out of the window. It looked such an exciting place to explore.

One day, Billy was staring at the rubbish tip, when he saw something gold-coloured gleaming in the sunlight. There, on the top of the tip, sat a brass lamp. Now, Billy knew the tale of Aladdin and he wondered if this lamp could possibly be magic, too. When his mother wasn't looking he slipped out of the back door, scrambled up the tip and snatched the lamp from the top.

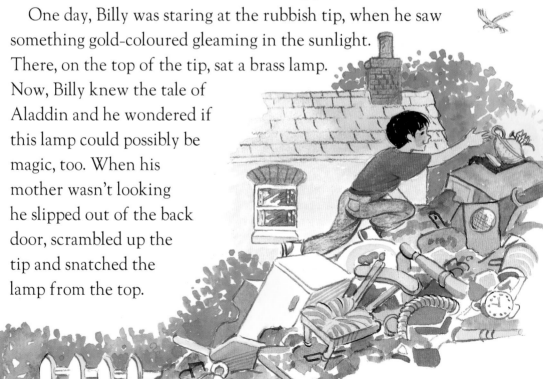

Billy ran to the garden shed. It was quite dark inside, but Billy could see the brass of the lamp glowing softly in his hands. When his eyes had grown accustomed to the dark, he saw that the lamp was quite dirty. As he started to rub at the brass, there was a puff of smoke and the shed was filled with light. Billy closed his eyes tightly and when he opened them again, he found to his astonishment that there was a man standing there, dressed in a costume richly embroidered with gold and jewels. "I am the genie of the lamp," he said. "Are you by any chance Aladdin?"

"N ... n ... no, I'm Billy," stammered Billy, staring in disbelief.

"How very confusing," said the genie, frowning. "I was told that the boy with the lamp was named Aladdin. Oh well, never mind! Now I'm here, I may as well grant you your wishes. You can have three, by the way."

At first, Billy was so astonished he couldn't speak. Then, he began to think hard. What would be the very best thing to wish for? He had an idea. "My first wish," he said, "is that I can have as many wishes as I want."

The genie looked rather taken aback, but then he smiled and said, "A wish is a wish. So be it!"

Billy could hardly believe his ears. Was he really going to get all his wishes granted? He decided to start with a really big wish, just in case the genie changed his mind later. "I wish I could have a purse that never runs out of money," he said.

Hey presto! There in his hand was a purse with five coins in it. Without remembering to thank the genie, Billy ran out of the shed and down the road to the sweet shop. He bought a large bag of sweets and took one of the coins out of his purse to pay for it. Then, he peeped cautiously inside the purse and sure enough there were still five coins. The magic had worked! Billy ran back to the garden shed to get his next wish, but the genie had vanished. "That's not fair!" cried Billy, stamping his foot. Then, he remembered the lamp. He seized it and rubbed at it furiously. Sure enough, the genie reappeared.

"Don't forget to share those
sweets with your friends," he said.
"What is your wish, Billy?"

This time Billy, who was
very fond of sweet things,
said, "I wish I had a house
made of chocolate!"

No sooner had he
uttered the words than
he found that he was
standing outside a house
made entirely of rich,
creamy chocolate. Billy broke
off the door knocker and nibbled at it. Yes, it really was made of
the most delicious chocolate that he had ever tasted! Billy gorged
himself until he began to feel quite sick. He lay down on the grass
and closed his eyes. When he opened them again, the chocolate
house had vanished and he was outside the garden shed once
more. "It's not fair to take my chocolate house away. I want it
back!" he complained, stamping his foot once again.

Billy went back into the shed. "This time I'll ask for something
that lasts longer," he thought. He rubbed the lamp and there
stood the genie again.

"You've got chocolate all around your mouth,"
said the genie disapprovingly. "What is your wish?"

Jimbo Comes Home

Jimbo the circus elephant was snoring away in his cage one night when he heard a strange noise. At first, he thought it was part of his dream. In his dream he was walking across a hot, dusty plain while in the distance there was the sound of thunder.

All at once, Jimbo was wide awake. He realized that he was in his cage after all and that what he thought was the sound of thunder was the noise of his cage on the move. Now, this worried him, because the circus never moved at night. He rose to his feet and looked around. He could see men pulling on the tow bar at the front of the cage. These were strangers – it certainly wasn't Carlos his trainer! Jimbo started to bellow, "Help! Stop thief!" But it was too late. His cage was already rumbling out of the circus ground and down the road.

Eventually, the cage passed through a gate marked 'Zipper's Circus' and Jimbo knew what had happened. He had been stolen by the Zipper family, his own circus family's greatest rivals! Jimbo was furious. How had the thieves got away with it? Surely someone at Ronaldo's Circus must have heard them stealing him? But Jimbo waited in vain to be rescued.

The next morning, the thieves opened up Jimbo's cage and tried to coax him out, but he stayed put. In the end, after much struggling, they managed to pull him out. Once he was out of his cage, he took the biggest drink of water he could from a bucket and soaked his new keeper! He refused to cooperate, kicked over his food and when he appeared in the circus that night he made sure he got all the tricks wrong.

"Don't worry," said Mr Zipper to Jimbo's new trainer, "he'll just take a little while to settle down. Soon he'll forget that he was once part of Ronaldo's Circus." But Jimbo didn't forget for, as you know, an elephant never forgets.

The other animals in Zipper's Circus had all been stolen from other circuses, too. "You'll just have to get used to it here," said one of the chimps to Jimbo. "It's not so bad really." But Jimbo decided he was going to try and escape.

One night, a mouse passed by his cage. "Hello," called Jimbo mournfully, for by now he was feeling very lonely and no one had cleaned his cage out for days.

"Hello!" said the mouse. "You don't look very happy. What's the matter?" Jimbo explained how he had been stolen and wanted to escape back to his own circus. The mouse listened and then said, "I'll try to help." So saying, he scampered off and soon he was back with a bunch of keys. Jimbo was astonished. "Easy!" said the mouse. "The keeper was asleep, so I helped myself."

Jimbo took the keys in his trunk and unlocked the door to the cage. He was free! "Thank you!" he called to the mouse, who was already scurrying away.

Jimbo's first thought was to get back to his own circus as fast as possible. However, he wanted to teach those thieves a lesson. He could hear them snoring in their caravan. He tiptoed up, as quietly as an elephant can tiptoe, and slid into the horse's harness at the front. "Hey, what do you think you're doing?"

neighed one of the horses, but Jimbo was already hauling the robbers' caravan out of the gate and down the road.

So gently did he pull the caravan that the thieves never once woke up. Eventually, they reached Ronaldo's Circus. Mr Ronaldo was dumbstruck to see Jimbo pulling a caravan just like a horse! Mr Ronaldo walked over to the caravan and was astonished to see the robbers still fast asleep. He raced to the telephone and called the police and it wasn't until they heard the police siren that the robbers woke up. By then it was too late. As they emerged from the caravan scratching and shaking their heads they were arrested on the spot and taken off to jail. "There are a few questions we would like to ask Mr Zipper regarding the theft of some other circus animals, too," said one of the police officers.

Mr Ronaldo, and Jimbo's keeper Carlos, were both delighted to see Jimbo back home again. And Jimbo was just as delighted to be back home. Then, Mr Ronaldo and Carlos started whispering to each other and began walking away looking secretive. "We'll be back soon, we promise," they said to Jimbo. When they returned, they were pushing Jimbo's old cage. It had been freshly painted, there was clean, sweet-smelling straw inside, but best of all there was no lock on the door! "Now you can come and go as you please," said Carlos.

And Jimbo trumpeted long and loud with his trunk held high, which Carlos knew was his way of saying, "THANK YOU!"

The Sleeping Beauty

A long time ago, in a land far away, there ruled the happiest King and Queen who had ever lived. They were especially happy because after years of hoping in vain, they had finally been blessed by the birth of a beautiful baby daughter.

The King and Queen were so happy that they decided to celebrate by throwing a huge banquet for their family and friends and all the most important people in the kingdom. As they sat down to write the invitations, a worried look crossed the Queen's face. "The Countess Griselda will be very angry if she doesn't get an invitation," she said to her husband.

The King's face went very pale for a moment. Then, he shook his head and said, "No, she must not be invited. Griselda is wicked and mean. I do not wish her to cast her eyes on our beautiful daughter." With that, they continued writing the invitations.

The day of the banquet arrived and all the most important people took their places in the Great Hall. Before the celebrations began, a line formed to pay homage to the little Princess Angelina, who lay sleeping in her cradle next to the King and Queen's thrones. Twelve people stood in line and one by one they stepped forward to give their gift to the sleeping Princess.

First, up stepped the good Lady Soprano, who touched the baby's throat with her forefinger and declared that the Princess would have a voice like an angel. Next came the Archduke Ernest and with a light touch on her forehead he vowed she would grow to be very wise. Next came the Duchess Rose, who stroked the baby's face and declared she would blossom into the most beautiful flower in the kingdom. One by one, the guests came forward and bestowed the gifts of patience, kindness, faith, grace, fortune, virtue, happiness and sweetness. With just one guest left to give her gift, there was a terrible noise outside the Great Hall and the huge doors were thrown open in a rage. In stormed the Countess Griselda. The Great Hall fell silent as she slowly approached the sleeping baby. The King and Queen jumped to their feet to protect their little one, but Griselda swept them both aside.

As they looked up in fear at Griselda, she turned to them and whispered in a hard, cruel voice, "I think you mislaid my invitation, but I have come to give my gift to the precious child anyway." As she bent over the child she cackled, "To this child I bestow the gift of absolute health until the day she dies." As relief showed itself on the faces of the crowd, she roared with laughter and bellowed, "Which is why it is such a pity she will not live beyond her sixteenth birthday!" The crowd was stunned as she continued, "A spindle shall be her end. A common peasant's spindle."

And she touched the tip of the middle finger on the baby's right hand. She then clapped her hands together and a great roll of thunder was heard, before a terrible wind swept through the open doors blowing out all the candles. When the doors were shut and the candles re-lit, Griselda had disappeared, leaving only her terrible spell behind her.

As the King and Queen wept, they did not see the final guest who had yet to bestow her gift. The Marquess Maria bent over Angelina and whispered, "I cannot take away the evil of Griselda, but I can give you the greatest gift of all. I give you the gift of love. On that terrible day to come you shall not die a death, but sleep, little one, sleep deep and peacefully as you sleep now, until love comes to rescue you." She placed her forefinger on the baby's heart and then was gone.

The King and Queen were in despair and they demanded that every spindle in the kingdom be destroyed. But they couldn't sleep a single night without worrying and a day didn't pass that they let the little Princess out of their sight for a moment.

Angelina grew and with every passing year she became sweeter and with every passing day she became more beautiful.

The day before Angelina's sixteenth birthday arrived and as the King looked at his daughter he felt a pang of sorrow, for he knew that he could not stop her destiny.

Her birthday arrived and for the first time ever the King and Queen allowed her to roam freely around the castle. The King had ordered a huge celebration to be prepared in the Great Hall for later in the day and Angelina had tremendous fun watching the cooks prepare delicious pies, pastries and cakes in the kitchens. She watched the servants making garlands of flowers and roamed through all the corridors to watch the preparations.

In a corridor off the Great Hall, she followed a trail of petals, winding first one way and then another, up and up into a turret in the castle that she had never visited before. When she reached the top, a door swung open and in the corner of the darkened room a little old lady sat spinning some yarn.

"Come closer, my child," she beckoned.

Angelina moved closer.

"Closer still," she urged.

When Angelina was close enough the old woman reached out to Angelina's right hand and pulled

374

it to the spindle needle. The Princess gave a gasp of pain as it pricked her middle finger and then she fell into the deepest, most peaceful of sleeps. And as she fell asleep, the whole castle fell asleep, too. The cooks fell asleep at the roasting spit. The horses fell asleep in the stable. The King fell asleep on his throne. Everything in the castle came to a complete and utter standstill.

The years passed by, and with every passing year the thorns that grew around the castle became thicker and higher, and the legend of the Sleeping Beauty spread to distant lands. As time went on, many brave princes tried to cut down the thorns, but not one succeeded and countless young men were lost forever in the forest of thorns.

Many years had passed before one brave prince awoke from a dream in which the angelic voice of a strange girl had called to him from a thorn bush. He asked his father the meaning of the dream, but the King shook his head and said it was best he didn't know.

But the following night, the young Prince once again dreamed of the strange girl and this time he saw the Princess deep in sleep but calling to be freed. The Prince was enchanted. She was the most beautiful girl he had ever seen and again he asked his father who she was. Again the King refused to say anything, but when the Prince's dreams continued and the Prince felt he would rather die than live without the Princess, the King relented and told his son of the sleeping Princess far, far away.

The Prince lost no time and set off on a voyage that lasted a year and a day. Along the way he heard tales of the princes who had tried before him and the fate they had met; some had been turned to stone, some had turned to water and others had simply vanished without trace, but none had succeeded.

The Prince finally reached his destination and stood outside the walls of the thorn forest. He knelt and said a prayer for all the lost souls who had tried before him and then he raised his sword to strike the thorns. In that instant, a vision of the Princess rose up to him and he was so overcome with love that he dropped his sword and tried to touch the vision. As he reached out he touched the thorns and as he touched the thorns, they turned into flowers in his hands. The further into the forest he went, the more the forest bowed down before him, until all that separated him from the Princess was a carpet of roses. The Prince raced past the sleeping horses, cooks and the King and ran up the stairs to where the Princess lay. He bent over her sleeping form and placed a single kiss upon her rosy lips. In that instant, she opened her eyes – love had set her free.

The cooks yawned at their spit and woke up. The horses neighed their yawns and woke up. The King yawned on his throne and woke up. Everyone in the castle woke up. When the Prince led the Princess to her father he cried with joy and granted him any wish that he could choose. The Prince asked for the Princess' hand in marriage and they both lived happily ever after.

You're Not My Best Friend

Gabriella Goat, Chicken Charlotte, Sam the Sheepdog, Penfold Pig, Sally the Sheep and Jersey Cow all lived on Willow Farm. In the late afternoon, when all the farm work had been done, they liked to meet in the paddock next to the farmyard to talk.

Gabriella was a very self-important goat, because she thought she was more useful on the farm than all the other animals. Not only did she provide milk for the farmer's wife to make cheese, but she also nibbled all the nettles and weeds and kept the farmyard neat and tidy. As far as she was concerned, that was much more important that just laying eggs or looking after sheep, or helping the farmer look for truffles, growing wool, or making milk.

Each morning, when Chicken Charlotte had finished laying eggs and all the other animals were still hard at work, she would flutter over the picket fence that kept the foxes away and strut over to visit Gabriella.

One very hot day, when the sun was shining down on the garden, Gabriella decided she and Chicken Charlotte should go down to the duck pond and soak their feet in the clear, cool water. Chicken Charlotte didn't like this idea at all! "I'm afraid I might fall in," said Chicken Charlotte. "I can't swim."

"You can't swim?" gasped Gabriella Goat. "How can you be any fun if you can't swim?" And with that, she turned her back on Chicken Charlotte. Gabriella thought about who else liked swimming and then smiled triumphantly. "Sam the Sheepdog can swim," she said. "In fact, sheepdogs can do lots of things chickens can't. Sam will be my very best friend."

Chicken Charlotte went back to her coop feeling very miserable!

Sam the Sheepdog had just finished chasing Sally the Sheep into the field when Gabriella Goat called out to him, "How about taking a break now and coming to the duck pond with me?"

Sam scratched behind his ear and panted hard as he thought about this. "Why not?" he said when he'd got his breath back. "It's a boiling hot day and I could do with a nice long swim to help me cool down."

Gabriella and Sam had tremendous fun all day splashing around in the water and at the end of the day Gabriella said to Sam, "You're my very best friend. Let's do this again tomorrow!"

Sam agreed. He was delighted that Gabriella liked him the best of all the animals.

The next day, Gabriella went to fetch Sam so that they could play. It was another very hot day and she was especially looking forward to a nice swim. Sam was in the field chasing Sally, but when Gabriella beckoned for him to come and play, Sam shook his head. "It's too early," said Sam. "I've got to make sure Sally grazes all this field and in any case most of the water has dried out of the pond and it's all muddy. The farmer won't like it if I get too dirty."

"What?" squealed Gabriella Goat in disbelief. "Whoever heard of a dog that didn't like mud? How can you be any fun if you don't like mud?" And with that she turned her back on Sam the Sheepdog. Gabriella thought for a while about who else might like mud and then smiled triumphantly. "Penfold Pig likes getting muddy," she said. "In fact, pigs like to do lots of things that dogs don't. Penfold Pig will be my very best friend."

Sam was too upset even to chase Sally around the field now and he lay down with his tail between his legs feeling very miserable.

Penfold Pig was snuffling around in the hot garden when Gabriella Goat found him. "Don't bake here," said Gabriella. "Come and roll in the mud with me."

Penfold Pig was delighted at this prospect and off they both trotted towards the muddy pool. They had such fun that Penfold wanted to do this again the following day, but Gabriella said that she'd had enough of basking now, and tomorrow she wanted to lie in the field and chew juicy grass. Penfold Pig was distraught. He didn't like chewing grass – he'd much rather eat pig-swill. Sadly, he told Gabriella Goat that he'd not be able to join her.

"Pah! Pathetic," she moaned. "You'll never make a good best friend if you can't eat grass." And with that she turned her back on Penfold Pig. She thought for a while about who else liked eating grass and then smiled triumphantly. "Jersey Cow likes eating grass," thought Gabriella Goat. "In fact, cows like eating grass all day long. Jersey Cow will be my very best friend."

Penfold Pig wallowed in the mud on his own and felt very miserable.

The following morning, Gabriella went to find Jersey Cow, who was just about to be milked by the farmer's wife. She told Jersey Cow her plans for the day. Jersey Cow said that she would be honoured to have Gabriella to talk to as they chomped and lazed the day away. "I'll be with you in just a tick," said Jersey Cow. "I need to be milked first."

Gabriella Goat stared at Jersey Cow and then turned and walked away without saying anything at all! "What's wrong with all these silly animals?" she asked herself. "Why do they always have to do something else first, or can't even do something at all?" And with that she decided to go alone to the juicy green field.

When Gabriella got to the field, she spied Sally the Sheep grazing away. "At last," she thought, "there's a creature that wants to do the same as me."

Sally the Sheep was very pleased to be chosen as Gabriella's friend and they spent the next hour talking and munching away in the heat of the Sun. Before very long, Jersey Cow came to join them. But Gabriella wouldn't talk to Jersey Cow, no matter how nice Jersey Cow tried to be.

"Friendship is all about giving and taking," remarked Gabriella to Sally the Sheep (so that Jersey Cow could overhear), "and being a very best friend means giving a lot. Jersey Cow can't even give up being milked for one morning. She's no best friend of mine."

Instead of looking miserable, Jersey Cow looked angry and when Jersey Cow moved off to chew some grass a little further away, Sally the Sheep followed her. Gabriella Goat snorted in disgust and then bent her head to chew some more. "Who needs friends anyway?" she thought. "They're no good to anyone."

But Gabriella Goat started to feel bored. She wanted to play a game. She wanted to play chase! Chicken Charlotte was the best friend to play chase with, so she decided it was high time to make friends with her again. As it was getting quite late in the day, all the animals were together in the paddock. Gabriella Goat could see Chicken Charlotte and so she skipped up to her to suggest a game. When she got close, however, Chicken Charlotte turned her back! Gabriella was taken aback and so she turned to Sam the Sheepdog. Sam also turned his back. As she looked at each animal in turn, they all turned their backs.